"You can't bear anyone who stands up to you!"

Serena accused Bren. "Well, let me tell you, you great brute of an Australian, that any girl can be the wife of a grazier if she gives her mind to it—only she'd have to be out of her mind to even consider it." Anger prodded her on. "I must have been out of mine to consent to this farce with you."

She felt humiliated. His punishing kisses had shown clearly that he didn't want her. She'd been a fool to think he might.

Suddenly it was too much to take. In tears, she brushed past him to her horse.

Within seconds she was riding as if the devil pursued her. Bren's warning cry was too late. Her horse was out of control, heading directly for the closed gate....

Other titles by
KATRINA BRITT
IN HARLEQUIN ROMANCES

Other titles by
KATRINA BRITT
IN HARLEQUIN PRESENTS

Many of these titles are available at your local bookseller
or through the Harlequin Reader Service.

For a free catalogue listing all available Harlequin Romances,
send your name and address to:

HARLEQUIN READER SERVICE,
M.P.O. Box 707, Niagara Falls, N.Y. 14302
Canadian address: Stratford, Ontario, Canada N5A 6W2

or use coupon at back of book.

The Hills Beyond

by

KATRINA BRITT

Harlequin Books

TORONTO • LONDON • NEW YORK • AMSTERDAM
SYDNEY • HAMBURG • PARIS

Original hardcover edition published in 1978
by Mills & Boon Limited

ISBN 0-373-02238-7

Harlequin edition published February 1979

Printed in U.S.A.

CHAPTER ONE

FROM the moment Serena and her friend Dee had arrived in Sydney they had both adored it. Wide-eyed with delight and wonder, they had gazed at the famous bridge and the fabulous beaches and had immediately succumbed to its charm. They had set out partly on impulse, partly on a whim for adventure and romance, to work their way around Australia. Dee, a domestic science teacher, was a superb cook, and Serena was a very able secretary and horse-woman, so they had reckoned on working their passage quite easily.

At twenty-two years of age they had considered it a wonderful idea to take a year off from their jobs to roam across a wonderful and magnetic country. Not for a moment had it occurred to either of them that anything could happen to upset their plans. But it had, in the form of a telegram for Dee saying that her mother was seriously ill. So Dee had left Sydney that morning to return home, not knowing when she would come back if at all.

Serena strolled along the hot city street in her lunch break feeling terribly bereft. They had been in Sydney for two months and had been fortunate to get jobs right away, Dee as an assistant cook to the chef of a high class hotel and Serena as a dentist's receptionist. Serena's job was only temporary until the girl whose place she had taken recovered from a car accident. But it was convenient, see-ing that they had only planned to stay on in Sydney to see the Royal Agricultural Show. The Show was to be opened in a few days' time and already the city was filling up with visitors eager to see one of the most important events of the year.

At the moment there seemed to be a surfeit of tall,

handsome, sunburnt men in white moleskin trousers, elastic-sided boots and broad-brimmed hats rubbing shoulders with the city-dwellers. Some of them were accompanied by smart, beautiful women who brought with them an aura of the outback.

Serena recalled how she had looked forward to seeing the outback. The plans they had made had been quite simple. From Sydney they were to move farther north to Queensland following the coast road and turning inland to eventually cross the border into Darwin. From Darwin. . . .

She was shaken rudely from her thoughts by a couple of teenage boys charging towards her. Before she could step out of their way one of them caught her a violent blow on her left shoulder as he raced past, swinging her completely off balance. A white-hot searing pain in her shoulder pitched her into what seemed to be a well of darkness. Then strong arms were around her, catching her as she fell, and a muttered oath came from a very masculine throat. Serena was vaguely aware of keen, observant grey eyes beneath a wide-brimmed hat and powerful shoulders shutting out the light before blackness claimed her.

A second white-hot pain in her injured shoulder, mercifully short, brought her round. Once again she was looking up into grey eyes, and a deeply tanned face. She was half sitting, half lying in the arms of the man who had rescued her from a nasty fall, and they were on the sofa of what appeared to be a luxurious hotel. Her rescuer had one arm around her and his hand was clasping the top of her arm near to the injured shoulder where the pain had come from. A feeling of nausea swept over her and sweat gathered like dew on her temples.

'Sorry I had to hurt you, but you put your shoulder out,' he said, gently wiping the moisture from her forehead with a large cool handkerchief. 'It's all right now. Putting it back wasn't the best way of bringing you round, but it did the trick.'

He turned his head as an elderly man approached bearing

a drink on a tray. He was obviously one of the hotel staff and was looking at Serena with some concern.

'The drink you ordered for the young lady, sir,' he said.

'Thanks.' Pushing the handkerchief into his pocket her rescuer, still keeping one arm around her, held the drink to her lips. 'You won't find this very pleasant,' he warned her, 'but drink it quickly and you'll begin to feel much better.'

Serena obeyed and suppressed a shudder as he handed the empty glass to the waiter.

'Not too bad, was it?' he asked, raising an attractive brow.

'No.'

Serena was beginning to feel better. She pushed back a short tendril of streaky blonde hair, noting his steady gaze, his crisp dark hair now minus the broad-brimmed hat and the powerful shoulders in the tweed jacket.

'Pain gone?' he asked.

'Yes, thanks,' she replied, and moved uneasily in his hold.

He continued to look at her intently. 'You brought it on yourself, you know.' His deep tones held impatience. 'You walked right into them. Didn't you see the kids making for you?'

'Do you think I would have walked slap bang into them if I had?' she retorted, taking umbrage at his tone. 'I happen to be above childish games. I'm twenty-two.'

His well-cut mouth quirked in amusement and his eyebrows shot up in surprise. 'I would have said you're no more than eighteen,' he commented dryly. 'So you can't blame the boys for trying to attract your attention. I can give you ten years, Miss. . . .' The grey eyes, rapier-sharp, switched to her ringless left hand.

'Serena. Serena Downs.'

She sat up away from his protecting arm and felt the colour flood her face. For some reason beyond explaining this very attractive man with his slow drawl, his virility and dominating charm disturbed her more than any man she had met. Moreover, he was looking down at her with the kind of mocking amusement which most girls would find irresistible.

'Bren Robart.' He relaxed his hold of her and extended a long lean hand. She clasped it lightly as his fingers closed around hers, and a curious sensation ran through her at his touch. 'I don't know if you're feeling better or if you're blushing,' he went on with a hint of satire, 'but the colour is certainly back in your cheeks.' His eyes wandered in a thoughtful way over her pleasing figure in the sleeveless cream linen. 'Here for the show?'

'You could say that,' Serena replied evasively.

'Not on your own?'

'You could say that too.'

'Not giving much away, are you?' he commented dryly.

'I'm sorry, but this happens to be my lunch break.'

She withdrew her hand from his warm clasp, aware that his dark grey eyes were having an alarming effect on her pulse, and made a move to go.

'So you haven't had lunch? Neither have I. Will you have lunch with me, Miss Downs?' he asked politely.

Serena bit her lip. 'I really haven't the time.'

'In that case,' he cut in, 'we can have lunch right here.'

'Here? At the hotel?'

'Motel,' he corrected her.

'But you don't have to give me lunch. Don't think I'm not grateful for your help, especially in putting my shoulder right. It feels fine now, it really does.'

Serena was not only aware that she was babbling, she was also aware that he was paying no attention to what she was saying. He was picking his wide-brimmed hat up from the carpet and putting it on his head. Then he signalled a passing waiter. While the man was approaching he rose to his feet and looked down at her.

'We'd better have lunch in my room,' he said. 'That way you can have a wash and brush up if you want.'

He turned to give an order to the waiter and Serena thought things had gone far enough. He had a way with him which made her feel completely powerless. She said firmly, 'I would like to make one thing quite clear—I'm not the kind of girl who's usually picked up in the street.'

His mouth quirked. 'In other words you're respectable. That makes two of us.' His tone cut her down to size. 'Shall we go?'

The next moment Serena was staring at him in consternation as she realised his intention to pick her up in his arms.

He reassured her with some amusement, 'Not to worry. Picking you up is becoming a habit.'

'A habit which I don't intend to encourage,' she replied, placing her hands on his arms as he would have put them around her. 'I'm quite able to walk, thank you. And don't get any ideas either.'

She was beginning to feel more like herself, and it was about time if she was to get anywhere with this very forceful young man. Meanwhile, he was much too close and unperturbed.

'I've plenty of ideas,' he told her with a charming smile. 'But they've matured somewhat more than those of the teenagers who deliberately ran into you by way of introduction. I don't go in for that kind of thing.'

'What do you do?' she queried coldly. 'Abduct your women?'

While she spoke Serena was trying to prevent his arms from going around her, a rather futile business, as she was discovering.

He grinned. 'It's an idea, especially as I prefer someone who's easy on the eyes and the arms, like you.'

Swinging her up into his arms, he was striding away with her before she could recover her breath. When she did they had arrived at his quarters. They entered a room of generous proportions where the decor was brown and gold offset by white. The outer wall of the lounge was all glass. The window drapes were a dull gold velvet and the carpet a lush brown. Gently Bren Robart put her down feet first on the carpet.

'How do you feel?' he asked. 'If you can make it to the

bathroom you'll find the cool water quite refreshing. I suggest you do that while I make a telephone call. By the way, everything reacts to push-buttons.' Taking her arm, he led her across the room to press a button near a door which opened to reveal the bathroom. 'It's all yours.' He made a half bow and stood aside for her to enter, then strode across the room to the telephone.

A wave of hot colour crept up beneath Serena's clear skin. He obviously did not stand upon ceremony where his lady friends were concerned. His tactics could be meant to take the woman by surprise, as he was doing with her. Well, he had certainly succeeded up to a point, she thought dazedly, watching him spin his hat right on target, which happened to be a chair near the door.

'Thanks,' she murmured with a hint of sarcasm.

'Don't mention it,' he replied, and picked up the telephone. His words into it were clear and concise. He was cancelling a lunch date, and she wondered if it was with a girl as she stood watching him.

As if feeling her gaze he replaced the telephone and regarded her with narrowed eyes.

'Feeling all right?' he enquired.

She gave a start, conscious of having been caught staring. 'Yes, of course. I was just wondering about you having a wash yourself.'

'After you, madame,' he answered lightly. 'You only need a refreshing dip under the tap. Leave bathing until your shoulder is really bedded in again. That way you won't have any further trouble with it.' He paused. 'All right now, isn't it?'

Serena nodded but did not move. 'Are you a doctor?'

He shrugged the question off as irrelevant. 'In the outback you become accustomed to doing most things, including taking instructions through the radio from the flying doctor. If it makes you feel any better, I've put shoulders back more times than I care to remember when my men have been thrown from their horses.' Here he threw in a lopsided smile for good measure. 'All of them were a hundred per cent successful.'

Serena turned to hide her sudden blush of embarrassment and went into the bathroom. She liked the white and
silver fixtures with the gold and brown towels and curtains
showing a sharp contrast of colour. Mindful of her lunch
break, she splashed cold water on her face and allowed it
to run over her wrists to cool her pleasantly from the heat
of the day, then she made up lightly to emerge from the
bathroom in good time.

Bren Robart made no comment at her sudden reappear-
ance as he turned from the window to take his turn in the
bathroom. On the threshold he paused.

'Lunch will arrive at any moment. Just let him in,' he
told her.

Serena never did remember what she ate during that
meal, but she did remember the management sending along
a bottle of champagne to help towards her recovery.

Taking it out from the ice bucket, Bren Robart read the
label and grinned at her.

'The best in the house. You ought to feel better after
this.'

Filling their glasses, he passed hers and raised his own.
'To your complete recovery.'

Serena touched his glass with her own and drank. 'I
mustn't drink too much,' she said lightly. 'I have to work
this afternoon.'

'And where is work?'

Putting down his glass, he removed the covers from the
dishes and began to serve the lunch. She told him and
went on to disclose the plans she had made with Dee to
tour the country. He listened while she told him about
Dee's mother being sick, then said casually,

'Are you planning on staying on in Sydney?'

'For the moment,' she admitted. 'I might even stay on for
quite a while. I like it here.'

He lifted a surprised brow and filled her glass again.
'What, Sydney?' he scoffed. 'You're only seeing it in the
spring. Wait until you experience the west winds blowing

in from the desert until the air is as dusty and gritty as the ground. In the winter that same wind can become intolerable. It gets through to your very bones like a knife, dries your skin and freezes you to the marrow. Then there are the winds from the sea, plus a few cyclones from that direction. Lots of people leave Sydney for the winter.'

Serena laughed. 'You're joking, of course. Why, it's a beautiful city—all this marvellous sun and the gorgeous colours of poinsettias and hibiscus in the parks. One of my friends here told me that there are weeks of endless sun here even in winter.'

He grinned. 'He forgot to mention the cyclones.'

She said, 'Who said it was a he?'

'With your face and figure it had to be. Besides,' his eyes mocked, 'he probably wanted you to stay in Sydney. My guess is that he's hoping you will.' He leaned back in his chair and smiled. 'Ever been to the outback?'

'No. I'd like to when Dee comes back.'

'Is she going to come back?' He drew a packet of cigarettes from his pocket and leaned forward to offer her one. 'Why not move on and let her catch up with you?'

'You mean to the outback?'

'Sure. Any good on a horse?'

He smiled again when she admitted to being a good rider. Then he put a lighter to his cigarette when she refused one. His next question surprised her.

'What exactly did you and your friend come out here for, apart from seeing the sights?' The pause was intentional. 'A man?'

The sudden heat in her face deepened the dark blue eyes which she lowered to her coffee. If he evidently thought that, why disappoint him? she mused.

'Could be,' she answered.

'How come that a pretty young thing like you is so starved of men that you have to come thousands of miles for one? This friend of yours, is she pretty too?'

'Dee is much prettier than I am. As a matter of fact I never stood much chance when she was around.' Serena's dancing eyes grew serious. 'We wanted to see something of Australia, that's all.'

'Then why don't you?'

She braved his disturbing regard. 'I might at that. Meanwhile I want to see the Agricultural Show.'

'Like me to take you around?'

'No, thank you.'

His eyes narrowed. Very carefully after sending a line of cigarette smoke into the air away from her, he asked, 'Got a date for every day of the Show?'

'No, but I'll be busy.'

Casually he shook ash from his cigarette on to an ashtray on the table.

'The Show is on for ten days.'

Serena nodded. 'I know, but I don't encourage pick-ups.'

'That's a bit strong, isn't it? If I'd allowed you to swoon at my feet I would still have acted the gentleman and picked you up. Surely you aren't holding that against me?' He tossed her a mocking look. 'I'm not suggesting anything immoral. As I said before, I'm perfectly respectable, and you'd have a good time with me and no strings attached either.'

Serena gave her attention once more to her coffee. While she had been aware of surprising him more than once during their conversation he had never once lost that air of self-assurance. That firm jawline indicated an inflexible will. His hands, immensely strong, held the cigarette in a light, deceptive hold and those broad shoulders were those of a man who had battled more than once against the elements and won. But apart from his superb physical structure, Serena liked his direct steady gaze, his sense of humour, and above all the fact that he instilled trust.

Furthermore, not only would he be a handy man to have around in case of similar incidents like the recent one that had brought them together, but it should prove interesting to get to know a man from the outback.

Keeping a solemn expression as though to emphasise her respectability, she agreed, 'All right. The Show opens in two days. But I can't see you on the first day—I have a date.'

'Fair enough. You can have dinner with me this evening either here at the motel or wherever you choose.'

Taken aback, she stared at him, found the grey eyes too magnetic and suspicions tumbled about in her mind. It occurred to her that some Australians could have descended from pirate ancestors who had settled there via the sea. The fact was borne in on her more profoundly because right now he was looking at her in the same manner that one of those pirates would have eyed a woman they had taken captive. Perhaps more firmness was called for, like letting him know that his offer to take her around did not exactly make him the piper who called the tune.

'Sorry, I'm afraid I can't manage this evening. I have to sort out things of Dee's to send on.'

'Tomorrow night, then.' He made it sound like a command.

Serena bristled at his tone. 'I'll give you a ring here.'

'Meanwhile you'll think up an excuse not to see me.' His sharp look seemed to penetrate her innermost thoughts. 'The least you can do is to give me the benefit of the doubt. We'll meet plenty of my friends and acquaintances at the Show who'll vouch for me.'

Serena dabbed at her mouth hastily with her table napkin and pushed back her chair, feeling rather foolish.

'I'll have to go or I shall be late. Thanks for the meal, and ... er ... for everything.'

'Don't mention it.' His voice was cool as he crushed out his cigarette and rose to his feet. 'I'm not surprised you're still unattached if you hold the males off back home like you have me. What are you afraid of?'

Serena had risen to her feet as he moved around the table to join her. His height put her at a disadvantage, besides making her feel very young and naïve.

'It's all right, you don't have to take me back to where I work—it's only a few blocks away.'

She was already on her way to the door when he said

quietly, 'You haven't answered my question.'

Serena gripped her handbag and spoke without turning round.

'You don't have to be afraid of a man simply because you don't make a date with him. I said I'll give you a ring.'

It was not until the bedlam of the city street hit her ears again that her senses began to function again normally, and she hurried back to work.

Her flat that evening was a welcome refuge, although it was strangely empty without Dee. She missed her alarmingly, missed her bright incessant chatter, her giddy reaction to dishy males, her fondness for strange foods, and lots more irritating habits which had suddenly become likeable and dear since she had gone. With memories of Dee still rankling Serena set about preparing her evening meal. Time enough later to gather Dee's things together and post them on.

The following day was particularly hectic, with half the city's increased population calling in for teeth extractions. Serena had a sandwich for lunch and left half an hour later than usual that evening with the burning desire to soak for ever in a lovely perfumed bath.

'Hello there!'

Ever since setting out for work that morning and even before that, when she had awakened to find the sun streaming into her room, Serena had pushed the thought of Bren Robart behind her. The sunlit street, the milling crowds around her faded into the background as she stared up into those clear-cut features with the ruthless jawline, steady eyes and teeth startlingly white against the dark tan of his face.

Perhaps she had hoped never to see him again, but deep down in her frightened heart she had known that she would.

'Hello.' The expression on her face belied her polite response, and she was aware of looking as limp as she felt after a hard day. 'Waiting for someone?'

'For you,' he replied laconically, and marched her along

the street to where his car was parked.

She held back as he opened the door of the car. 'I'm sorry, I'm too tired to go out this evening. Besides, I'm not dressed for it.'

'A few minutes under the shower will change all that,' he said equably. 'Hop in.'

He almost lifted her into the car, slammed the door and went swiftly round to slip into the driving seat beside her. At her flat he suggested staying in the car while she got ready, but Serena insisted upon him coming in. After all, his company was preferable to an evening without Dee.

His wide-shouldered frame brought the dimensions of the lounge down somewhat and she felt rather than saw those steady grey eyes roaming around the neatly carpeted room with its easy chairs, vases of flowers and a small bookcase.

'I've only apple juice to offer,' she said apologetically, 'other than tea or coffee.'

He lowered his long length into one of the comfortable chairs and stretched out long legs.

'I'll wait,' he replied. 'We can have something later.'

The shower was invigorating, but Serena did not linger. She slipped on a smart tailored dress in oatmeal, clipped the smart leather belt around her trim waist, and tied a pretty paisley scarf loosely around her slim throat to look casually chic. Then stepping into bronze court shoes, she picked up a matching handbag and gloves, slung an oatmeal topcoat over her arm and was ready.

Bren Robart was leafing through a glossy magazine and looked up in surprise as she walked into the lounge. His gaze roved over her slim belted figure, the shining hair and the wide blue of her eyes.

'That was quick,' he drawled. 'Or couldn't you wait to get me out of your apartment?'

Serena laughed, a low sweet pleasing laugh that made him look at her with a crooked smile. 'That's better. You're quite something when you shed your inhibitions. Could be that being fenced in by conventions has cramped your style.'

He moved easily to her side as he spoke and took her arm.

'I had no idea that my style was cramped, but my stomach could be. I've just realised that I'm hungry after only having a sandwich for lunch. I was sorry for my boss. The poor man was rushed off his feet,' she said demurely.

She watched him extend a long arm to open the door and wondered if her giddy reaction was owing to his nearness or the fact that she was hungry. He seated her in the car, slammed the door and went round to take his seat beside her. When her pulse had stopped working overtime, Serena sat back in her seat and willed herself back to normal. Even so the man beside her churned her emotions considerably until she began to wonder about it. He had said that she had been cramped in by conventions. Well, no one could say that of him! He was like some bionic man, virile, immensely strong, and full of confidence.

She asked as casually as she could, 'Are you a cockie or a grazier?'

He chuckled. 'You've been doing your homework! I'm a grazier. You could say my ancestors were cockies generations back. They were British and came out to farm in the fertile valleys near to Adelaide in the eighteenth century. Later they moved on to Queensland to take up farming in a bigger way. Now I have relations all over, even in Sydney here.'

'Must be cosy,' she replied as they sped along past a plethora of motels and petrol stations. 'There seems to be a surfeit of motels around.'

'Lord yes. They've certainly gone to town on them. But we aren't going to eat in one. We're going to a favourite place of mine, the Kangaroo Inn.'

At the speed he put up they were soon cruising along a tree-lined road and making for a car park beside a sprawling cedar-built place backed by gum trees in gardens ablaze with deep red poinsettias and hibiscus. The expert way in which he slid into a certain place in the car park gave Serena the idea that she was not the first girl he had taken there. Glancing at the disturbing profile and the dark jacket outlining wide shoulders it was easy to assume that he had only to crook a brown finger to have a choice of any girl around.

The oak-studded cedar door opened on to a sea of carpet. Serena left her coat at the hat check counter and Bren led her up half a dozen steps to a cosily lighted bar. To their right was an archway leading into a dining room where smart waiters moved around discreetly between immaculate tables. The bartender addressed him cordially, with a smile for Serena.

'What will it be, Mr Robart?' he asked. 'The usual?'

Bren grinned. 'I don't think my friend here is the beer-drinking type.' He looked down at her in query, and she hated herself for blushing.

She said, 'Anything will do. A tomato juice, I think, please.'

Bren's smile was openly mocking. 'Playing safe?'

Her smile was demure. 'A girl can't be too careful in a big city.'

His lips twitched. 'Don't down it all at once,' he teased.

The food and service was excellent. Serena ate with enjoyment and finished on a replete note with the best coffee she had ever tasted. Bren had proved to be an entertaining companion, talking in a leisurely relaxed way which left lulls in the conversation in which to enjoy the food. He said little about his homestead apart from the fact that it was called Tamura and that it was quite big. Serena deduced this to be an understatement since she had discovered that he was not given to boasting.

After the meal he sat back in his chair to enjoy a cigarette.

'Enjoyed it?' he asked, exhaling smoke into the air away from her.

She nodded. 'Enormously, thanks.'

'So have I. You don't talk a man to death and you have

a delicious way of talking and laughing that I find charmingly discreet. In the outback you become part of the great silence and the first impression you get upon arriving in the city is that the noises tend to deafen.'

Diplomatically, she asked, 'Do you find it dull at times back home?'

'It would be,' he admitted. 'That is if one had the time to. Mostly I'm always ready to hit the hay at night after a day or so out mustering with the men.' He paused and leaned forward to tap the ash from his cigarette into an ashtray on the table. 'Mind you, we have our moments—barn dancing, card playing and entertaining.'

'And drinking?'

Bren grinned. 'I must watch it,' he scoffed. 'Like I said, you've been doing your homework. The boys let themselves go when they come to town. As for me, I've sown my wild oats, and it's been fun.'

'And you haven't married?'

Serena lowered her eyes hastily, regretting the words as soon as they had been uttered. There was something about her disturbing companion that made her wary of probing too deep into his personal life. A surface friendship was the best, since they were to be but ships that pass in the night, as it were.

'Tell me about the swag you carry in the outback,' she tacked on swiftly. Her smile was most disarming.

He accepted the switch in the conversation lazily and obeyed amiably.

'The swag is really a bedroll. The thick canvas sheets have a flap pocket to hold blankets, clean clothes and personal belongings. The whole thing is held together by two strong leather straps. You simply spread out the canvas and roll up in a blanket.'

He went on to talk about the barn dances, barbecues, bush race meetings and flips in a plane to visit neighbours and friends. His deep brown voice held her enthralled as she listened to him with wide blue eyes.

Presently his mouth began to twitch and he drawled,

'You look about ten years old with that wide-eyed look in your very blue eyes. The outback isn't all romance—it's real hard work. We work hard and we play hard.'

Her face was the colour of a wild rose. 'I can imagine that. You must think me awfully dumb.'

He said whimsically, 'There's nothing wrong with you that time won't put right. I like you as you are. Unfortunately we have our quota of bad men here who will like you that way too. Upon reflection I think it will be sensible for you to make tracks for home, since your friend has gone.' He jabbed his cigarette into the ashtray provided with some force as if some thought had annoyed him and pushed himself to his feet. 'Shall we go? You've had a hard day and you need your beauty sleep.'

Serena was puzzled at his sudden change of mood, but was inclined to agree with him as the warm interior of the car caused her eyelids to droop without volition.

'Wake up, sleepyhead!'

The deep tones penetrated her unconsciousness, and she opened her eyes to sit up, blinking sleepily. Bren had left his seat to come round the car to help her out. They had arrived at her flat.

'The Agricultural Show opens tomorrow,' he commented on the way to her door.

'I know. I have a date tomorrow night after work.'

'So you said.' His tone was noncommittal as he held out his hand for her key.

The silence between them dragged somewhat as he opened the door. With deep compunction, Serena recalled that he had given her a delightful evening and that the least she could do would be to ask him in for a nightcap. So she said, 'Will you come in for a quick coffee?'

He hesitated, slowly returned her key and let his grey eyes roam leisurely over her bright hair, the dark blue of her eyes and her sweet, soft mouth which he found to be almost irresistible. Then just slightly his mobile mouth thinned and his expression was grim. Once again Serena wondered what had caused the change in him.

'You'd better drink your hot milk and go to bed like a good little girl,' he said. 'That way you won't come to any harm.'

Serena was still working that one out as she heard his car drive away. Then very slowly she began to prepare for bed.

CHAPTER TWO

THINGS were quiet at work the next morning and Serena put it down to the opening of the Show. So at lunch time she went along to see what was happening. There was a restaurant and a milk bar there and she chose the latter in order to have a quick snack which would give her more time to take a look around the exhibits. The time went on wings and she had only toured the fruit and flower displays before it was time to return to work.

A girl stood waiting for her outside the office, someone she had never seen before who regarded her with cool, unfriendly eyes.

'I'm Eunice Bailey,' she began without preliminaries. 'I believe you've been taking my place while I've been away.'

Taken by surprise, Serena felt her heart lurch, aware that her future in Sydney would be decided in the next half hour. Then cordially she held out her hand.

'I'm Serena Downs,' she smiled. 'I hope you're feeling much better.'

The girl was about to reply when Mr Hanna appeared.

'Ah, Miss Bailey!' he cried in surprise. 'I didn't expect to see you quite so soon. How are you? I must say you're looking well.'

'Quite well, Mr Hanna. In fact I'd like to start work next Monday if it's all right with you.'

Mr Hanna, a wiry little man with a receding hairline, took off his spectacles and polished them while looking nervously at Serena.

'It seems I have to dispense with your services, Miss Downs,' he said. 'I shall give you a month's salary in lieu of notice, of course, and I intend to give you an excellent reference. I really don't know what I would have done without you. I'm very sorry.'

Serena smiled at him warmly. 'Thanks, Mr Hanna, you've been very kind. I'm glad I was able to help out. I've enjoyed it enormously—and I did accept the job on a temporary basis.'

She made her way to her flat that evening still in a sense of bewilderment. While she had expected the job to fold up in the near future, there had been a slight hope that it would last long enough to give her time to decide upon future plans, so it was with some regret that the parting of the way had come so abruptly without warning. Mr Hanna had been more of a friend than an employer, kind, courteous and not in the least demanding. She would miss him.

Looking ahead, there seemed little point in her getting another job and staying in Sydney. With Dee, everything around her had held a kind of enchantment, but now that enchantment had waned. Wistfully she thought of Dee and wished futilely that they could have gone on with their plans. She missed her friend—missed the bond of affection between them. Now she would miss Mr Hanna as well. Her footsteps dragged and a painful dryness stung her throat as she asked herself the question. It had to come sooner or later.

Did she want to go on alone? Bren Robart had told her in no uncertain tones to go home. Maybe she ought to take his advice. The flat seemed very empty when she walked in with a large paper bag of groceries to the kitchen. Steak and onions were frying merrily when the door bell rang.

'Hi, Serena!'

A freckle-faced twelve-year-old girl sporting a ponytail of dark hair burst in wearing sneakers, jeans, and an anorak. The look of rapture on her face as she breathed in the appetising smell of cooking lifted Serena's flagging spirits.

'Hi, Katy. Will you lay the table while I finish the steak? I'm cooking a few chips with it because it'll be quicker than doing vegetables. All set to go to the Show?'

'You bet!'

Katy shrugged off her shoulder bag, hooked it on to the back of a chair and followed Serena into the kitchen.

'It is good of you to take me ten-pin bowling when you must have had heaps of offers from young men wanting to take you. I'm glad you're staying until your friend comes back.'

Serena dropped chip potatoes into the deep fat and gave her attention to the steak. She said, 'I might not be staying.'

Katy dropped a fork and swung round with dismay. 'But why? Dee is coming back, isn't she?'

'I don't honestly know. In the meantime I have to eat, and my job is finishing this weekend.'

'Gee, I'm real sorry!'

'So am I, but it can't be helped.'

Katy picked up the fork and polished it on a cloth. Laying it on the table, she smiled and said cheerfully, 'But you're sure to find another job. Mom and Pop say it wouldn't be right for you to roam around Australia on your own. Best to wait until Dee comes back.'

'We'll see.'

As she dished up the meal Serena almost wished that she had not promised to take Katy to the Show. But the poor mite had so looked forward to going and her parents were not able to get home from work soon enough to take her. Bren Robart telling her to go home and the folding up of her job had upset her so much that she needed time to think. But the sight of Katy putting away the steak and chips followed by two helpings of cheesecake soon made her smile.

Everybody appeared to be going to the Show that evening and Serena and Katy joined the crowds passing through the entrance. The time went on wings, with Serena enjoying the ten-pin bowling as much as Katy. She had no idea how long Bren had been watching them. He was leaning back against a pillar just behind them when she saw him. Her bowling had not been at all bad up to then, but it was no good from then on.

His whimsical gaze had moved on to acknowledge Katy

after greeting her, and that young lady was only too glad to accept his invitation to go to the milk bar for refreshment. Bren bought her favourite ice cream concoction and Serena settled for a milk shake. He had nothing himself. Katy was busy with her treat when he said in an undertone, 'Why didn't you say you were bringing the youngster? I could have taken you both out to dinner and brought you along here afterwards.'

Serena sipped her milk shake. Since his appearance on the scene she was feeling ridiculously happy without knowing the reason for it.

'I don't think Katy's parents would like to think she was going out with a strange man.' She gave him a swift glance as he stood leaning back nonchalantly against the milk bar while they sat on high stools. 'Besides, we mustn't be late back. You'd enjoy yourself more going for a drink with your friends.'

His eyes narrowed. 'You're living dangerously, my sweet,' he murmured. 'What time are you planning on leaving?'

She dropped her gaze and her fingers closed tightly around her glass. The timbre of his deep voice, his disturbing presence was whipping up all kinds of emotion inside her. A glance at her watch told her that it was nine-thirty.

She said, 'The place closes at ten, so we might as well leave when we've had our drink.'

'I'll take you both home. I suppose you want to go to bed early for work in the morning,' he said. 'How was it today?'

'Not too bad—in fact we had an easy day.'

It was on the tip of her tongue to tell him that one late night would not matter and that she would go out with him to some night spot. He had, no doubt, looked forward for months to a visit to the city and he had been kind to her. But a warning bell pulled her up sharp. To her relief he did not press her to go out later. Instead he looked along the bar at Katy and smiled charmingly at the moustache of ice cream around her mouth. Then he deliberately winked. Katy was completely captivated by him and she sat between them in the Land-Rover when he drove them back to the flat. He dropped them off, lifted a lazy hand and left Katy speechless with admiration watching him drive away.

'Wow!' she exclaimed. 'Poor Serena. Did you ditch a guy like that for me?'

'I never ditch anybody. Now hurry in or your mother will be worrying about you. And thanks, Katy. I enjoyed it.'

'Sure?' Katy asked. 'I know you could have gone with Bren, so you needn't tell me otherwise.'

Serena kissed the small woebegone face warmly. 'Now, Katy, you have to believe I had no idea that Bren would be at the show this evening. I wanted to take you, otherwise I wouldn't have suggested it, now would I?'

Katy shook her head. 'It's been lovely, and I do hope you don't leave us.'

Serena ate her breakfast with the dismal feeling of being at a crossroads with no idea which way to take. In the bright morning sunlight all the places she wanted to see beckoned. Besides, there was Bren Robart. Not that she would see much of him since he was only in Sydney for the Show. He had not mentioned seeing her again and she decided to forget all about him.

She was kept busy all day with little time to think, and if she was disappointed because he was not outside waiting for her when she went back to the flat, she tried to tell herself that it did not matter. There were more important things on her mind. The telephone rang as she was putting the kettle on to boil. It was Bren. He was calling for her in an hour to take her to the Show. For precious moments Serena stood as though in a daze, then with a bubble of laughter she made for the bedroom to choose a dress.

She chose an apple green silk jersey top and a cream pleated skirt. Both would go well with her oatmeal top-coat, and were suitable for touring the Show. Lightly making up her face, she pondered over the attractive man from the outback, knowing that her friend Dee would have gone overboard for him in a big way. Serena had to admit she found him exciting in a way that was far different from any other dates she had had in the past. But then he was an Australian and the first she had dated on her own. Previously, along with Dee, she had made a foursome with whatever dates they had had since coming to Sydney, and on two occasions the young men had been English students just passing through.

Serena was ready when Bren arrived and in case he thought her too eager, her greeting was skilfully casual. Nevertheless, her heart somersaulted as he escorted her to his car. Wearing his brilliant smile, he moved beside her with the loose-limbed grace of a feline animal. His dark suit added to the charm of a bronze tan laid on by the sun, wind, and rain of the great outdoors.

'Been busy today?' he asked after he had set the car moving.

Now was her chance to tell him about her job folding up, but something kept her silent. It was impossible for her to account for her reason for not telling him except that their friendship seemed to be overlaid by a prudent doubt.

They were of two different worlds. Everything about her belied her inexperience. She was at a disadvantage, giving him the right to take the initiative where she was concerned. And she was still so shy of him that she accepted whatever he decreed. From her point of view this was wrong, but as long as she did not become too involved there was no cause for concern.

She answered him lightly, 'So-so.'

He tossed her a glance with raised brows. 'What about that day off that you're supposed to have?'

Her face coloured—the penalty one had to pay for subterfuge, she told herself less lightly. Her honest and direct nature rebelled against such practices, but there it was.

'I'll let you know,' she replied evasively, and changed the subject. 'By the way, Katy likes you,' she added.

For a moment there was an awkward silence while Bren swung the car around a bend to join a line of traffic to a car park.

'She's a nice kid,' he commented. 'What are her parents like?'

Serena relaxed feeling on safer ground. 'Wonderful. They work at the local hospital. Her mother is a nurse, her father an ambulance driver. They were both on duty last night, so they couldn't take Katy to the Show.'

His tone was cynical. 'Those rare birds, a happily married couple.'

Serena took him up sharply, not caring for his cynicism. 'Not so rare. Normal sensible people do sometimes make a success of marriage.'

He agreed with a touch of irony. 'Would you describe yourself as a normal sensible person?'

She laughed. 'I'm afraid I put that rather badly. I made marriage seem terribly ordinary when it can be the most beautifully satisfying thing in the world.'

'Is that so?' He swung the car into the car park, chose a place near to the exit and slid expertly into the space provided. Then switching off the engine, he turned towards her with an arm on the wheel to regard her intently. 'Do you speak from experience?'

Serena laughed again. Her face had a saucy and animated glow. Slowly Bren's eyes roved over her clear sparkling blue ones, her tender sensitive mouth, her amazingly thick dark lashes, and the cool creamy texture of her slim throat.

'Goodness, no! I know lots of people who are happily married. Most of my friends are.'

'Good for them,' he drawled equably. 'So you will, no doubt, follow in their footsteps and live in a state of connubial bliss for the rest of your life?'

'I didn't say so.'

'Why? Afraid to take the plunge?'

'What makes you say that?'

He shrugged wide shoulders. 'Let's go back to these normal sensible people you mentioned earlier. Wouldn't you agree that, while they had a certain kind of unity, they never actually reach the heights of happiness that lifts one entirely out of this world?'

Serena wrinkled her smooth forehead. 'I don't understand. You mean passion?'

His eyes narrowed. 'It's easy to see that you've never really been in love.'

The short time that ensued was fraught with tension, which Bren was the first to break by turning abruptly to open his door.

The crowds milling into the Show were eager to see the evening's events, which included polo, log felling and a rodeo. This evening it was a rodeo, and fortified by a hot meat pie washed down by a beer, Serena and Bren joined the Show.

Bren had seated her at an improvised bar, looked down at her indolently from his graceful height and asked her what she wanted to drink.

'Lemonade? Coke?'

His regard, slightly mocking, had riled her. It relegated her to the position of a sixth-former at school.

'A beer, please,' she said sweetly.

His dark eyebrows lifted above eyes glinting with amusement. 'Does madam prefer a small one or a large one?'

Serena had lifted her chin. 'A large one, of course.'

He ordered two large beers and she met his steady gaze over the rim of her brimming glass. He was laughing at her, and in that moment she hated him. The drink was ice cold, sharp and not at all bad. She did not have to drink it all. Or did she? The pie was hot, savoury and delicious.

Bren was smiling as at some secret thought when they joined the Show. Then Serena forgot him in the excitement of watching the rodeo.

The thrill of the buck-jumping was hilarious and exciting. It was very skilful entertainment and Serena enjoyed the pick-up teams as much as the participants in the rodeo. Their job was to ride in and pick up a rider after he had done his stint, providing he was not still on the horse. Two men rode in, one to pick up the rider and put him on his feet, the other to catch the horse.

As Bren had said, many of the people at the Show knew him, those taking part in the rodeo and spectators too. When they hailed him they cast a cursory glance at Serena which gave her the impression that it was not unusual to see him with a girl-friend.

Indeed, several beautiful girls with escorts greeted him warmly, but their glance her way had been speculative. Around nine-thirty, Bren suggested them making a move to avoid the mass exit. They were on their way out of the grounds when a strawberry blonde running slightly to fat laid a plump hand on his arm.

'Hello, Bren,' she said. 'I don't suppose you've seen Kerry?'

'No, I haven't.' He narrowed his eyes in a gentle regard at the girl's anxious face. 'Ask around. He could be any-where.'

'I have, but no one seems to know. I've never known him miss a Show before.'

The girl's full lips quivered and Bren patted a plump arm. 'Don't worry, Rose. He'll turn up. Don't be too possessive when he does—that's no way to hold a man. I'll let you know if I see him. So long.'

They were at the place Bren had chosen for a meal when Serena asked,

'Who's Kerry?'

Bren shrugged carelessly. 'A young fool of a jackeroo.'

'Does he work for you?'

'He does.'

'Tell me about him.'

'There isn't much to tell. Perhaps I ought to tell you that a jackeroo is a kind of general dogsbody who's expected to work all hours at the beck and call of the particular home-stead who employs him.'

'You mean he's a kind of servant?'

'You could say that. But it's a job very much sought after. He has a good life as almost one of the family, and

even takes the place of the boss when he's away by helping to look after callers.'

'Then what's he doing at the Show when you're away?'

'Because the Show is one of the highlights of the year
and we all come to see it. The boys need to let off their
high spirits once in a while. They work all the better for
it later.'

'I see.'

Indeed, Serena saw all too clearly that the boss, like his
boys, came to town to enjoy himself. With a lump feeling
like the size of an ice bucket in her throat she managed
to smile at him across the table. She wondered what kind
of a girl he had picked up at last year's Show. Someone
like herself perhaps who had literally fallen into his arms?
He had probably taken her to this very place for dinner,
and he was looking at her now as he had done many times
to other girls.

'What do you fancy?'

The rich brown voice cut across her thoughts and she
blinked at him, aware of being in a brown study. The
menu she held did not make much sense to her jumbled
thoughts, so she said the only possible thing:

'You choose.'

Bren rubbed the side of his nose, studied the menu, then
ordered. But Serena's mind was not on food. She was
learning more about her companion and was not sure
whether she cared for it. To her he had appeared to be the
type who instilled trust, to repel merely by his appearance
and behaviour any suggestion of loose living. Or was that
too strong a term? Just because he took girls out it did not
mean that he was no good.

On the other hand, he was a virile, healthy man with
a man's normal desires, tough as they come and ruthless
with it. He was part of a big, ruthless country. Meanwhile
he was watching her with a shrewd eye and what he saw
in her face must have irritated him, for he spoke with his
voice on ice.

'You don't trust me even now, do you?' he demanded.

The face she raised was slightly flushed. Drat the man! He really did have a disconcerting way of reading her thoughts, and she despaired of ever being able to completely relax in his company. It took quite an effort to gloss over her doubts.

She drew in a dry lip. 'I don't think I would have come out with you if I didn't trust you.'

The waiter came at that moment before Bren could react to her reply. When he had gone Bren lifted his glass and though he smiled charmingly his grey eyes were speculative.

Whether or not it was the excellent meal or Bren setting himself out to be charming, Serena was never sure, but it could account for the feeling of unreality which persisted as they left the inn. In the scented dusk the harbour lay wreathed in diamonds of light against a velvet backcloth of sky. There was no hint of a wind and the air had the caress of spring blossoming into summer.

Bren was quiet, and the feeling appeared to be mutual as Serena lay back against the well sprung upholstery of the car.

'I wonder if Rose found her Kerry,' she murmured. 'I do hope she did.'

She turned in time to catch his enigmatic glance, and he spoke with a cynical derision.

'Sentimental little thing, aren't you? For your information, Rose will be lucky if she doesn't find him. Kerry has a wandering eye attached to a cool calculating brain. So don't waste your sympathy in that direction,' he said offhandedly.

'I hate to see people unhappy, and Rose had all the appearance of it,' she said stubbornly.

'Any chance of me getting some of that sweet sympathy if I admit to being unhappy?'

He drew on to the grass verge at the side of the road and switched off the engine. When he shifted sideways to look at her the air was suddenly short of oxygen and it hurt her to breathe.

She made an effort to be flippant. 'I can hardly see you crying over Kerry.'

'I should hope not,' he snorted. 'We don't have that kind around here.'

Serena stared until the penny dropped. Then she laughed, a low husky sound of real mirth.

'I'm sorry,' she said, mopping the tears of mirth from her eyes to find him grinning at her.

'Heard from your friend yet?' he enquired.

She shook her head. 'Why do you employ this Kerry if you don't like him?'

'He's a good worker, and as long as he behaves himself on my property that's everything.'

'But you were really sorry for Rose,' she persisted.

'I like the girl. Why shouldn't I?' He glared suddenly at the changing expression on her face. 'And don't look at me like that, damn it!'

'Like what?'

'As if by admitting I like the girl I must have had an affair with her. I'm going to take you home before I lose my temper.'

Suiting the action to the word, he started the car and sliding out on to the road set off at speed. He did not speak on the way back to her flat, while Serena drew farther away from him into her corner, looked at that strong dark angry profile and wished he would keep away from her in the future. By the time they reached her flat she could not wait to get away from the big man behind the wheel. Maybe it was just as well that she had not told him about her job folding up. It simplified matters all round.

As she wearily shed her clothes for bed Serena realised that it was not more than a week since Dee had gone, yet it seemed like years. In fact the real reason for their coming to Australia was becoming obscure. If she was to continue with her plans for seeing the country it was essential for her to pull herself together, live up to some kind of pattern like regarding disturbing men like Bren as ships that pass in the night. That was exactly how he would regard Serena Downs, for she was no femme fatale whom he would find it hard to forget.

Brushing her hair, she viewed her face dispassionately in the mirror. Her fair skin was one of her best features. One could say that her nose was delicately cut, that her mouth was pretty, her blue eyes wide spaced and eloquent and her blonde hair striking in its streakiness. But all in all she was no different from dozens of other girls who tripped lightly along the hot Sydney streets on long golden legs.

Too restless to sleep, she switched off the light and wandered to the window. Outside the dark shadows of night held an alien and disturbing influence, a strange fascination. There was so much to see, to explore, the chance of a lifetime to see a country that was growing fast into something exciting and important in the world. And here she was poised on the threshold.

Her rent was paid up until the end of the month, and she had enough money to see her through until her next job, wherever that might be. So she would go, leave Sydney and continue on her way as though Dee was with her. Maybe with Bren Robart behind her she would begin to feel normal again.

CHAPTER THREE

SINCE making up her mind on her future plans Serena felt more settled and resolved to take the loss of her job philosophically. Her morning at work passed happily, for the patients were mostly children having fillings and checks. Serena warmed to the children as much as they warmed to her. Those who came alone were given some of the children's books and she would sit and talk to them while they were waiting to take their mind off what they had come for.

She had taken a sandwich lunch in the park, deciding it was wiser to keep away from the Agricultural Show in case Bren was around. It might have been the sun or the disturbing awareness of his presence in Sydney and the chance of bumping into him that brought on a headache. Strolling back to work, she reflected that it was strange how one accepted change. Yesterday at this time she was returning to find the end of her job looming. If she was a little apprehensive at what lay ahead, it was only natural. No one embarking on an unknown adventure alone when she had expected to have company could be entirely free from small fears.

The office, when she entered it, was clinically cool. Mr Hanna was already there in his white jacket going through the files with a brisk businesslike movement. Finding what he was after, he closed the drawer and bestowed a warm smile upon Serena.

'I was wondering if you would care to have dinner with us this evening,' he said with a twinkle. 'I've told the wife a lot about you—how good you are with the children, and how sorry I shall be to lose you. She's quite intrigued and would like to meet you.'

Quiveringly aware of her headache, Serena wanted to

refuse, but he was regarding her with such a fond expression that she felt near to tears.

'Of course,' he went on as she hesitated, 'if you have another engagement we shall understand. It is a bit short notice, but we're going out to a friend's tomorrow night and the following night I have to go to a business meeting.'

'I'll come with pleasure.'

She spoke from the depths of pain and resolved to take something for her headache. But that evening when she had washed and run a comb through her hair the headache had gone. Maybe it had gone without her volition since Bren had not telephoned or shown up at her flat. Well, so much for that. She could forget him.

Serena had never met Mrs Hanna, had never tried to visualise her, so the woman came as a pleasant surprise when she walked into the lounge of her employer's home to see a good-looking woman of about forty-five with a golden tan and dark hair free from grey.

She came forward with an exclamation of pleasure. 'So nice of you to come, Miss Downs. I practically bullied my husband to ask you. I've heard so much about you, and I couldn't bear the thought of you leaving without meeting you. I happen to be English myself, so we shall have much to talk about.'

The Hannas' son, a bright young man of twenty-two, made up a foursome for dinner. He was studying to be a doctor and there was just a hint of pride in the look Mrs Hanna gave to her son as she told Serena this. The evening, to Serena, was both enjoyable and just a bit poignant since she was soon to part from a delightful family.

She was back at home in bed when the telephone rang, and she lifted the receiver, half asleep.

'Serena?' demanded the deep voice. 'I tried to contact you earlier, but you were out. Bren here.'

As if she didn't know, when her heart was beating overtime. 'Hello, Bren. Yes. I have been out.'

'To the Show?'

'No, just dining with friends.'

'Interested in polo?' he asked.

'I don't know. I've never seen it played.'

'Then here's your chance. I'll pick you up tomorrow night. We're going to the Show. Shall I pick you up at work?'

Serena thought rapidly of the danger of him calling to pick her up at work since in a day or so she would no longer be there, and she did not want him to know, at least until she had thought about it, that her job was about to come to an end.

'No. You see, I might get off a little earlier and I'd much rather go home for a wash and change first.'

'Then I'll call for you around six-thirty?'

'That will be fine.'

She put down the receiver with a trembling hand. Even the mere sound of his voice reduced her to pulp. Not for a moment did she permit herself to question the wisdom of such a date with a man she was trying so hard to forget. After all, her stay in Sydney was coming to a close and it was only sensible to savour its attractions with a first-class guide and companion. Bren was entertaining in a nonchalant way, lazily amused at her wide-eyed appreciation of all that was strange and new, and above all he took care of her as if she was something precious. She was not, of course. It was just the way he was. He would have been the same with Rose or any other woman he was taking out.

His gallantry, his virile masculinity held her under its spell. His strong dark features, his steady grey eyes, his compassion for a girl like Rose who was in love with a bounder all tended to reach out to her heart until she seemed to be a part of him herself. Since recognising her feelings for him, Serena had teetered between despair and ecstatic dreams in which Bren and no other man could ever take part.

When he called for her the following evening she was ready and tried not to look too starry-eyed. In the car he told her carelessly that he was taking part in the polo that evening at the Show, but he had made sure that she would get a good seat from where he would collect her when the game was over. He grinned, seeing her look of surprise that he was taking part, and told her she was his good luck mascot.

Bren behind the wheel of a car with his white smile was calculated to set any woman's heart haywire, but in white jodhpurs, high riding boots and silk shirt open to show a firm strong brown throat, and that devil-may-care look on his face, he was dynamite to her shaky heart. During the game when her eyes lost track of Bren they alighted upon the beautiful high-bred horses taking part. How she would have loved to ride one! The horses her mother had kept at their riding stables were nothing to be compared in beauty to these lovely creatures who appeared to enjoy the thrills of the game as much as the riders.

Bren scored one of the goals and made it possible for another two to be scored for his side, which eventually won the game. To celebrate they went to a restaurant, where champagne and lobster were called for. The delicious meal, and sharing his victory with the knowledge that her presence had helped, made Serena marvel at the happy and alive person she had become.

Their conversation was light, and punctuated with ready laughter. They were two people delighting in each other's company and snatching moments from the gods which she knew would never return again. The small warning bell alerted by the common sense inside her was ignored. It was useless to remind herself that her knowledge of the man was practically nil, that he was filling in his time pleasantly to suit himself, that those heart-lurching looks he gave her were no different than those he had given to other women.

While she had no idea of the game he was playing, it was clear that it had gone from the playing stage with herself. She was utterly lost in the enchantment of his deep voice, his nonchalant, amusing charm, and that masculine arrogance that became lost in the protective cloak he held around her. In her delirious happiness it was not possible for her to think of the future in concrete terms. If she did she might run away and forgo these precious times with Bren that would brighten her barren future lying ahead.

He took her out every evening until the end of the Show, always calling for her at her request at her flat. That way he did not discover about her job ending. He never invited her to his place again and he always dropped her at her door. His manner throughout, his behaviour, was impeccable, almost as if he did not intend her to misconstrue his motives. But for Serena his presence was enough.

It was the night after the Agricultural Show had closed. Bren had escorted her home after taking her to a night club which she had enjoyed immensely. Unlocking her door, he leaned against the frame dangling her keys in his fingers, and said lazily, 'I'm going away tomorrow. I'll be gone a week. You aren't moving out yet, are you? Decided about going home?'

Serena lowered her eyes from his probing gaze and said awkwardly,

'No, but I could make up my mind to leave on the spur of the moment.'

His smile was sardonic. 'Tut, tut! I'm surprised at you leaving your employer just like that.'

She was poised for an instant to shoot through the doorway in order to avoid further awkward questions and tried in vain to tell him about her job being no more. But no sound came from her dry throat and it was difficult to keep quiet as he stood there regarding her mockingly. All she could think was that this could be the last time she would see him, and the knowledge made her feel curiously numb. Trying to imagine Sydney without him was like dying a little, as through her fogged mind came the thought that he would find her gone on his return. If he did mean to return. It was possible that he had planned on a quiet exit like herself with no complications.

Serena bit her lip. It hurt too much to think or even talk any more. Managing to lift the corners of her mouth into the semblance of a smile, she said, 'The rush for extractions and fillings is over now the Show has finished. It's been a bit hectic, so if you'll excuse me, I am rather tired.'

For several moments Bren looked at her pale strained face and dark blue eloquent eyes through narrowed lids. Then he reached out a brown hand to ruffle her hair.

'Past your bedtime, is it?' he drawled.

The arrogant assurance was back in his manner. He was never without it for long. For an unguarded moment Serena felt only sympathy for the woman he was going to see— and she was sure that it was a woman. Just as she was sure that Serena Downs was not the first woman to receive his offhand treatment.

She was aware that he straightened from the door frame, then he was bending down to bestow a kiss on her hair.

'Pity to tease you.' He put her key in her hand and kissed that too. 'See you when I come back. So long. Take care!'

Maybe it was better to say goodbye to a beloved city and a beloved one at the same time, Serena told herself sadly the following morning. Although it would leave a wound that was more deep and painful, wounds healed in time.

Leaving her bed to pad to the window on bare feet, Serena looked wistfully out at the harbour gleaming like molten metal in the sun's rays. The trees were tender in leaf and birds trilled in full-throated song among wisteria, jasmine and lilac in the garden below. She sighed as she recalled her first chore, which was to write and tell Dee that she was moving on and would forward her address.

After breakfast she packed most of her things, plenty of jeans, a beautifully tailored pair of moleskin jodhpurs, tailored shirt tops, evening dresses and sweaters for the cold evenings. The hardest part was to come when she said goodbye to her friends. Katy was tearful, and even the present Serena gave her was small comfort for losing her friend.

The day wore on, to end on a sad note as she got back to her flat with the good wishes of her friends ringing in her ears. That evening she cleaned through the flat to save time the next morning. That way she could take a bath on rising, have breakfast, and face a minimum of chores before she left.

Preparing breakfast for the last time was a chore prodded with memories. Certainly her stay in Sydney had enriched her life in that respect. Furthermore, the Serena Downs who was leaving was a far different girl from the one who had arrived months previously. She thought whimsically how often in the past Dee's love affairs had amused her. Her friend had fallen in and out of love with a delicious abandon that left her remarkably unscathed. Yet here she was, reeling from a light affair which Dee would have taken in her stride. What more of a fool could one be?

This deep feeling in her heart was for a man who at that very moment had probably forgotten all about her. Different facets of him flashed across her mind—kind, charming, sardonic, cynical, whimsical, protective, and arrogantly enigmatic. Which was the real Bren? With a man so expert at hiding his true feelings it was impossible to tell. The very strength of his character lay in the fact that he would never permit his true feelings to be seen in public. They would always be battened down.

His future would be all planned out since he had made up his mind about what kind of wife he would choose. Serena could imagine the kind, an unusually beautiful girl with a rich dusky tan emphasised by the colourful background of the outback. She would be good at most things and so magically right. But these thoughts only tormented and did nothing to temper her love for him. It burned in a deep glow inside her until it became an ache. Idiotically, and because she could not help it, she would go on loving him even though it meant facing a barren future of futile regret.

At half past eight everything was packed and she was ready to go when the doorbell pealed. The caller was evidently impatient, for the second peal followed quickly after the first and went on and on. Wondering who it could be at such an early hour, Serena hurried to the door and opened it.

'Oh, hello!' she gasped weakly on breath regained.

'Aren't you going to ask me in?' Bren drawled sardonically. 'Not got a man in there, have you?'

Serena moved in the aperture to stop him peering in at her luggage.

'I'm very busy. . . .' she answered, and broke off.

'So I see.'

He had walked into the room, putting her aside gently to observe her suitcase and the pristine freshness of the room. His voice was dangerously quiet.

'Going places?'

Serena felt her face go hot. She gave him a stricken look.

'But weren't you going away?' she said.

'Sure. And you're making a getaway in case I come back,' he said grimly. 'Why didn't you tell me about your job with Hanna folding up?'

'I didn't think it was important. Why haven't you gone away as planned?'

He pushed his hands into his pockets and replied impatiently, 'Because I'm here instead. Now what is all this?' He nodded at the suitcase and all the evidence of the room that indicated her quitting the premises.

'I'm moving on, that's all. I'm going on with our plans until Dee catches up with me. It's as simple as that.'

His mouth tightened and the grey eyes darkened with anger. 'Do you realise what you're letting yourself in for?' he demanded tersely. 'Why not let the whole thing drop and go home like a good little girl? No good can come of you carrying on alone.'

Serena tilted her chin. 'How do you know? I'm quite capable of looking after myself and earning my way around,' she retorted with spirit. 'I'm an experienced secretary and I can handle a horse successfully—I've done that from an early age. Both are qualifications that should see me being accepted wherever I go.'

Serena moved into the room while Bren leaned against

the door frame as though blocking her exit. Grasping the back of a chair to give her confidence, she faced him pale-faced.

He went on impatiently. 'From what you've told me about your friend I'll guarantee she's already dating some enterprising young man back home and has no intention of returning.'

Serena regarded him witheringly. 'If I know Dee she's with her sick mother, whom she adores.'

'And her mother probably adores her daughter in return, which means that the woman won't want her daughter to put thousands of miles between them again by coming out here.'

'So what? Is it any of your business?'

He said bluntly, 'I dare say you're angry about my interference. But it's as well to remember that you're not in the U.K. now. You're a fool to take such a risk, travelling alone.' His mood changed and he gave the impression of being tolerant against his will. 'Why not go back home and settle down with some nice young man?'

Serena gripped the back of the chair. Very quietly she said,

'Thanks for your advice. What I do is no concern of yours. I've met only kindness since coming to your country and there's no reason why I shouldn't continue to do so. I'm sorry that what I propose to do doesn't meet with your approval, but there it is. You've been kind to me and made my stay here in Sydney a memorable one, so don't let's spoil it by parting as enemies. I'll say goodbye now—I have to catch my coach.'

For what seemed an eternity to Serena Bren continued to regard her much in the way of a kind of mathematical problem he had some difficulty in solving. Uneasily she lowered her eyes to the white knuckles resulting from her grip of the chair back. He was so dear, standing there larger than life, and her heart ached at the thought of parting from him. It would have helped enormously to have been able to read his thoughts. One could only conclude that he was thinking fast, readjusting himself to this new situation and coming to his own conclusions.

At last he straightened indolently from the door frame and said,

'Since you're determined to go I'll take you to your coach. I take it you're on the point of leaving?'

She said defensively, 'I'm only going as far as the Pacific highway. I can manage.'

He bent down to pick up her luggage as if he had not heard, and telling herself that this was Bren who would always have his own way in things, Serena turned to gather up her other belongings through a blur of tears. He was well ahead of her when she caught him up, but he did not look at her as he put her into the seat of the big car to slide in beside her.

She sensed his anger as he put on speed, a clear indication of his wish to be rid of her as soon as possible. She could not blame him.

She said shakily, 'I'm sorry, I ought to have told you about my job.'

He presented her with a tanned unyielding profile. 'So am I. I thought we were friends.'

'We are,' she replied, utterly miserable.

'We are?' he echoed, his mouth lifting in a sardonic slant. 'You could have fooled me! You sure have a cock-eyed way of regarding friendship. Do you usually clam up on your friends and run out on them?'

'No, I don't. I didn't want you to know about my losing my job because I wasn't sure about taking another here in Sydney. I wanted time to make up my own mind without any friendly advice from anyone.'

'And what's so wrong with friendly advice?'

'I told you I didn't require any.'

'You mean from me?' he asked, adding with a trace of acid, 'Or did you consider my advice as not being in your own interests?'

She gave him a startled look, said indignantly, 'Such a thing never occurred to me, and I. . . .' She broke off and glanced through the windscreen of the car to give a sharp exclamation at the way they were taking. 'You're going the wrong way!'

Bren did not move a muscle. 'Strange, I thought you were the one going the wrong way. Calm yourself, I'm not abducting you. We'll stop presently and have a little talk.'

'But I don't see. . . .' she began as he ran the car off the highway on to a grass verge.

Switching off the engine, he turned with an arm on the wheel to look at her. 'Stubborn little cuss, aren't you?'

Serena stiffened. 'One could say that you are as well.'

'Agreed. May one ask what you have lined up in these plans of yours?'

'I haven't a job, if that's what you mean.'

'Then I have a proposition to put to you.'

'A proposition?' Serena echoed weakly. 'What kind of proposition?'

'Don't look so scared,' he said sharply. 'I'm not planning to seduce you. I happen to be going on a visit to an aunt of mine of whom I'm very fond. Unfortunately, she's keen for me to marry her adopted daughter.'

She said, feeling rather shattered, 'Is she beautiful, this girl?'

'Some would say she was.'

'But not you?'

'I didn't say so.' He smiled. 'The point is if I take a girl-friend along it could scotch any idea of my hitching up to this particular dame.'

Serena moistened dry lips. 'But if she's young and beauti-ful. . . .' she began.

His laugh was derisive. 'And I suppose that means I should marry her and live happily ever after. You've been reading too many romances, little one.'

'What's the snag?' she asked curiously.

'This girl has had too much of her own way. She needs a lesson.'

'And you want to teach her one?'

He lifted wide shoulders. 'Could be. What do you say

to going with me? I can introduce you as a friend of mine who's seeing some of the country. Aunt Julia would make you very welcome.'

Serena gazed at him, at a loss. While her head was urging her to hurl a cold negative, her heart was saying something entirely different. It was reminding her how kind he had been to her, that it was mean to refuse him a favour in return.

She said quietly, 'Is it so important to you that you have to take a girl-friend with you?'

'Very,' laconically.

Again that hesitation while he stared through the windscreen ahead as though giving her time.

'You've been very good to me and I. . . .' Bren did not allow her to go on.

'I want you to do nothing out of gratitude. I had as much enjoyment from our friendship as you did. And I'm not forcing you to make a decision along those lines.'

The wall she had erected between them earlier was now there again. He had not turned his head, but she knew his mouth had tightened and that he was miles away from her in warmth and friendliness. Serena could not bear it.

'I'll go with you,' she said.

What did it matter that from now on life would be ten times harder because she would have his companionship and a taste of what it would have been like to really be his girl-friend?

'Good girl!'

He squeezed her shoulder and Serena winced with the feeling that he was squeezing her heart. From where she was sitting he looked like a man in love with a spoiled girl who was going to set about taming her in his own way. For a start he was putting himself out of her reach by bringing along another girl. Judged by the set of his lean jaw this beautiful spoiled girl was in for a few surprises and some rough treatment. Yet in that moment Serena would have given all she had to be in the unknown girl's shoes.

They were well away on a long stretch of road when

Bren began to talk about their destination.

'We have a couple of hundred miles to cover to the Cockatoo, Aunt Julia's place. The station comprises some of the finest wheat and sheep in the country. I'm usually expected after the show in Sydney to play polo. It's a great get-together of friends and neighbours. There are barbecues, dances and the usual celebrations we Aussies delight in.'

'Will—will her daughter be there?'

'I have no idea. All I know is that Sadie was to have come to the Show in Sydney, but as far as I know she never showed up.'

'Is that why you're sore with her?'

He tossed her a white grin. 'Lord, no! The next time Sadie keeps a promise will be the first.'

But you're going after her, Serena thought hollowly, and gave her attention to the passing scenery. Hills dense with gum trees rose stark against a vast blue sky and the sun glinted down on the vast Hawkesbury river as they crossed it to head north. Attractively built homesteads began to appear, surrounded by huge areas of grassland housing sheep and cattle. Gradually as the sun gathered strength the car became an oven. Serena began to steam, her head felt muzzy and her throat dry, as Bren sped on. At last after what seemed an age of flashing scenery a cluster of buildings came into view to form a bush town of several small hotels, the usual post office-cum-general store and a saddlers.

Bren slowed up to pull in at a trim café at the end of the street. Around it yellow wattle was standing up against the hot dry land. They walked up steps under a sign announcing 'Sam's Place', and entered a neat room set out with smart check cloth-covered tables with built-in chair cushions to match. Bren was greeted like an old friend by the proprietor, who came forward to shake his hand and be introduced to Serena.

Their lunch was excellent, thick succulent steaks and

lamb chops followed by a mouthwatering display of tropical
fruits. The coffee was good and Serena allowed it to flow
gratefully down a dry parched throat. Over her second cup
Bren studied her thoughtfully.

'How are steaks back home?' He drawled as he lit a
cigarette.

She grimaced. 'Awfully expensive.'

'We'll have to feed you up while you're here. That
fragile look is no good for the outback.'

'I'm healthy enough,' she retorted.

He jeered openly in a mocking, teasing way. 'Australian
women are beautifully robust. Some of them drink iced
beer and like it.'

Serena said vexedly, 'Iced beer doesn't make a woman
more feminine.'

He grinned and she was aware that he was only teasing.

'That streaky hair natural?' he enquired politely.

'Of course it is.'

This time Serena kept her cool. He was trying to rile
her, and that smile showing strong white teeth, a smile
which did not on occasions reach those dark grey eyes,
annoyed her as he hoped it might. She prickled in spite of
her resolve to keep cool.

'Comparing it with your beautiful Australian women?'
she asked shortly.

His eyes rested thoughtfully on the hair. 'No, I like it.
You're the kind who'll still look beautiful when you're old.'

'Who said anything about being old? I have lots of
things to pack into my life before then. I would think that
the climate here plays havoc with a woman's complexion.'

Bren nodded and said softly, 'But there are compensa-
tions.'

Her face flooded with colour and his laugh made her feel
so alien that she wanted to hit him. He belonged under
wide blue skies, hot sun and scattered homesteads where it
was not unusual to drive a hundred miles for a cuppa with
a friend or neighbour. Serena Downs was *de trop*.

'Never mind. Sam is evidently taken up with your hair—

he's been staring at it for some time. And now here he is coming over,' Bren grinned.

Serena turned to see Sam's white-jacketed figure moving in their direction. His round ruddy face beamed with the warm hospitality that pervaded the place along with the pleasant aroma of good food. His look sobered somewhat when he reached their table. His voice was low and meant for their ears alone.

'Sadie passed through here three days ago on her way to the Cockatoo. All burned up, she was. Didn't even wait until the last day of the Show. Seems she couldn't find you since you weren't staying at your usual hotel.'

Bren's lips twitched. 'Stranger things have happened,' he confided with a wink at Serena.

Sam gave a knowing grin. 'And about time too, if you ask me.'

His admiring look at Serena was strangely gratifying, and by the time they were well on their way again Serena had been recalling one of those stranger things that Bren had referred to.

'That motel you carried me into that day when the teen-agers pushed me over wasn't the place you'd planned on staying, was it? Sam mentioned a hotel, not a motel.'

She looked at his profile, willing him to glance her way, but he did not.

'Is it important?' he queried coolly, looking straight ahead.

'Not really, only I'm curious as to why you did it. You acted on the spur of the moment, didn't you, when I said I hadn't the time to lunch with you.'

'Maybe I thought you'd bring me luck.'

'You can do better than that,' she scoffed. 'Anyway, what amazes me is how you knew the layout of a strange room so well.'

'I've been to Sydney often enough to use similar places. My recent visit to Sydney was not, as you seem to think, a kind of once-yearly Sunday school outing. I make numerous business trips during the year as well.'

Very slowly Serena said, 'I hope you aren't one of those wealthy graziers one reads about.'

He looked at her speculatively. 'Why?'

'Because I would have steered clear of you had I known that in the beginning. We wouldn't mix. I only have what I earn.'

'Would you feel better if I told you that compared with my near neighbours who happen to be wealthy, I'm very poor indeed?'

'But I'm sure you won't be for long,' she said. 'I mean, these business trips you make must produce results or you wouldn't make them.'

'That's very clever of you. I can see I'll have to take you on as my partner.'

She smiled and said demurely, 'I'm too fragile, I believe you said.'

He grinned. 'I can see I'm going to enjoy your company still more as time goes on. What about you?'

Her answer was guarded. 'I have to be on my guard since you're playing on your own ground.'

'You don't pull any punches, do you?' Bren jibed, and gave his attention to the road ahead.

CHAPTER FOUR

SCENERY, however strange and intriguing, tends to pall on a long journey. Serena had sat up eagerly when she saw the kangaroos and commented on their look of helplessness as they danged their short front paws. Bren's comments when she had called them darlings were not very complimentary, however.

'But they have to eat,' she insisted.

'So do we,' he replied.

The speed Bren put up sending the big car zooming along the straight road did not bring the horizon any nearer. There were distractions for Serena, a flock of budgerigars rising startled from the shrub, their green breasts presenting a colourful sight, and bigger birds with pink breasts and grey wings which Bren told her were galahs.

'They're a species of parrot and are very often to be seen in the bush,' he said, and viewed with mocking amusement the look of enchantment in her dark blue eyes.

It was late afternoon when he pulled up at the side of the road to lean over to the back seat to pick up a picnic basket.

'Just a quick snack of sandwiches and coffee, then we have to push on.' He looked at her sudden smile with the mocking, maddening approach he seemed to use expressly for her. 'And don't tell me it isn't welcome. You've been quite good, no incessant chatter or complaints about the heat and dust, or enquiries as to our next stop.'

Serena lost her smile and wished he would stop treating her like a schoolgirl.

'You forget,' she retorted as he handed her a cup of hot steaming coffee from a flask, 'Dee and I planned to travel the country the hard way. We toughened up for it months before back home by going into the country and taking long hikes during the weekends.'

He grinned. 'Good for you, but Australia is a different country altogether. Here you have to be aware of snake-bites and possibly scorpions. How do you fancy living in the outback with your nearest neighbour miles and miles away?'

Serena swallowed part of her coffee and accepted a sandwich. 'I wouldn't know until I'd tried it. I tell you one thing—I miss Dee dreadfully. We've always been together, had dates together and generally laughed our way through life comparing our favourite males.'

He said dryly, 'Tell me about your favourite male?'

She munched, then laughed softly on something remembered. 'I haven't any favourite male at the moment that I care to discuss. Tell me about your Aunt Julia. Will she resent me because of her hopes for her daughter concerning you?'

'As a matter of fact she'll make you very welcome. She's a good sort and can usually see things for what they are.'

He went on to talk about the Cockatoo and what a good job Julia was doing in running it since her husband had died two years before. Serena sat very still and hanging on to every moment in the intimacy of his company. A sweet smile curled up her mouth and lit the dark blue eyes. She would not have to let him down. She would have to match her personality with Julia and Sadie, who would be disliking her pretty thoroughly. But it did not daunt her. The challenge would be something to bite on during her visit, which she hoped would be short.

When they set off again the light was fading. In the distance the hills were silhouetted darkly against a changing sky. White cockatoos wheeled, their wings looking like scraps of paper in the gathering dusk. And the road stretched before them again into the unknown.

Gradually the rays of sunset filled the car with an eerie light that left Bren's profile etched in a bronze mould. There were cattle grazing in paddocks and Serena's eyelids were heavy. She awoke to find her head against Bren's shoulder. A moment of awareness struck, forcing her to sit up, dazed with sleep, to see him slide out of the car. The headlights were lighting up a wire gate and she knew that they were on the Cockatoo station.

There were other gates at intervals, then finally the car was approaching a long, low rambling building, the Cockatoo homestead. They had arrived. Lights blazed from high windows encircled by verandahs to offset the sun and a background of cork trees formed a kind of oasis in a sea of paddocks.

Serena left the car on what felt like two wooden legs as she straightened stiffly to hear the barking of dogs. The cold crisp night air made her quiver after the confined heat of the car and she breathed in deeply, fully awake to the wholesome smell of cattle and earth. A door opened at the top of verandah steps letting out a stream of light along which two big dogs bounded joyfully to greet them. The next moment Serena felt hot breath on her face followed by a slobbering tongue, and the dogs dropped down from them at Bren's stern words of command.

She fondled their silky ears while Bren took the luggage from the car boot and a woman appeared in the doorway of the house. The light from within formed an aura of brightness around her blonde head as she came forward to greet them, a slightly built woman who moved swiftly and gracefully to show her pleasure in an expansive smile.

Bren closed the car boot and laid a careless arm around Serena.

He said, 'Aunt Julia, this is Serena Downs. Serena, my favourite aunt, the charming owner of the Cockatoo. I want you two to be great friends.'

If Julia was surprised she hid the fact well. Her smile was warm and welcoming as she took Serena's hand. Serena liked her instantly, warming to the firm clasp of her hand, the frank, friendly gaze. For a woman in middle age with the added burden of doing a man's job, Julia was remarkably well preserved. Her blonde hair was neatly styled and her figure trim and neat in a smart evening blouse and skirt.

'Delighted to meet you, Serena,' she said in a rich low-pitched voice. 'Come along indoors. I'm sure you must be tired after such a journey from Sydney, and I know Bren. He's indefatigable!'

She could have added that her nephew gave nothing away, but diplomatically, she asked no questions. It was her own intuition that suggested something was amiss. The girl was exhausted and rather bewildered, but this was no time to ask questions.

Serena was given a room at the far end of the front façade of the homestead which opened through french windows on to the verandah. Going by the sound of voices and music coming from the living quarters it was evident that a party was in progress. It was probably being given in honour of Bren's arrival, so it looked as though she had to wash and change and present herself to back him up. She felt desperately tired, but after a session in a warm bath finished off by a cold shower, she felt much better.

She had just finished dressing when there was a peremptory tap on her door and Bren practically filled the doorway. At the sight of his clear-cut features, the thick dark hair in lazy waves and the grey eyes looking at her so enigmatically, her heart performed its usual feat, something between a plunge and a somersault.

'Everything all right?' he asked, his eyes roving over the streaky blonde hair falling in a soft gleaming wad across her forehead, the dark blue of her eyes echoed in the simply cut dress of blue jersey. 'I thought we might join the others together.' A gleam flickered in his eyes and was banished swiftly. 'That dress brings out the colour of your eyes. I like it.'

His expression had changed, it was whimsical, almost teasing. Serena pulled herself up sharply, reminded herself that their association had to be kept entirely platonic and murmured a polite reply. In less than no time they had plunged into a warmly lighted room to meet a crowd of people. Their entrance was the cue for everyone to turn round in their direction, glass in hand. The laughter and chatter stopped as at the drop of a hat and someone struck a chord on the piano at the far end of the room. Bren went a dull red beneath his tan as they sang, 'For he's a jolly good fellow.'

'Easy now!' he protested.

Someone put drinks into their hands and they were suddenly swamped by a happy chattering crowd.

'You can't blame them,' Julia put in on an aside after Bren had introduced Serena to all and sundry. 'You've never brought a girl-friend to the Cockatoo before, and we're all agog. Wait until Sadie comes! She's over at the Belmores' and we expected her back for the party.' She regarded her nephew shrewdly. 'You know she was looking for you in Sydney at the Show?'

Bren shrugged. 'So what? As far as I'm concerned Sadie only turns up to suit herself. I was at the Show with Serena.'

'Probably why you didn't see her,' Julia said dryly. 'You weren't at your usual hotel, I believe.'

'No.' Bren lifted a tantalising brow. 'Should I have sent you a wire?'

Julia laughed, a laugh without mirth. 'I know you always do exactly as you please and we poor women are too much in love with you to wish it otherwise.'

'Of course we are!'

The vision who had uttered the last words flung her arms around Bren's neck and tiptoed up to kiss him. When he refused to bend down to meet her lips, her kiss landed on his chin. The girl was not abashed at this treatment, for her voice was meant for all to hear.

'And where were you at the Show?' she demanded. 'How dare you use another hotel and leave me high and dry!'

'Motel,' Bren corrected her mockingly.

The girl, elegantly dressed in a halter-necked almost backless evening gown in apricot chiffon that brought out the satin-tanned smoothness of features framed by dark hair, regarded him with mock severity.

'And what were you doing there?' she asked coyly, keeping her arms clasped loosely around his neck. 'As if you'd tell me!'

Somehow Julia had inserted herself between Serena and Bren so that he had to reach around his aunt to draw her forward.

He said lightly, 'Why not? Meet my girl-friend, Serena Downs. Serena, I want you to meet Sadie MacNeith.'

Like a sleepwalker slowly awakening, Sadie stared at Serena open-mouthed.

'I see,' she said at last. Her laugh served to bolster up the front she was putting on and Serena admired her for it, also for the way she cleverly avoided taking her hand. 'Maybe I would have met you two sooner had I not been so busy myself. Where's Kerry?'

Sadie turned to look around the room and Serena, conscious of Bren's arm around her, suddenly felt that arm contract when the girl drew a young man in his twenties forward.

He had a foreign look about him, slim, dark-haired, of medium height with a certain attraction in the long olive face and black eyes. He moved forward with the fluid grace of a panther as his eyes held Serena's in a brief moment with open admiration.

She thought, a womaniser if ever I saw one! Out for all he can get.

Sadie was saying, 'I hope you don't mind me commandeering Kerry. We had a great time together, didn't we, darling? See you later.'

Thrusting her arm behind Kerry's, Sadie took him away, much, it seemed, to the relief of that young man, who was avoiding Bren's steely gaze.

If anyone looked capable of murder at that moment it was Bren, Serena told herself shakenly. Her heart quailed at the malevolent look he bestowed upon the young man's back as they moved away. It was only too clear that he was resenting him bitterly because of his association with

Sadie, which could only mean that he loved the girl.

But Kerry was not at the dinner table where hothouse blooms vied in splendour with silver and cut glass. Serena noted this as she sat next to Bren, who was the target of jocular teasing from the males. Where had he met Serena, and were there any more like her still around? But Bren sat through it patently at ease. Sadie, seated by Julia, confined herself to her immediate neighbours, and if her laugh was over-loud and frequent, no one seemed to notice it except Serena, who felt sorry for the girl.

Poor Sadie, she thought, and how relieved you'll be to discover that Bren loves you after all. She had not missed Julia's tense and anxious face either and knew she sensed the undercurrents stretching across that snowy white tablecloth from Sadie to Bren.

Serena was not clear about the rest of that evening. She heard herself giving the appropriate answers to eager questions about her native country and managed to smile until her mouth muscles ached, though her world had collapsed about her. At last she was safely back in her room telling herself that once she had recovered from the proof of Bren loving Sadie, she would doubtless find sufficient courage to go through with Bren's plan until he had his heart's desire.

Masculine voices outside her window on the verandah awakened Serena and she lay for several moments listening to the deep timbre of Bren's voice. He sounded angry and the answering voice was sullen.

'You've got a nerve to come out here instead of going back to Tamura. And don't tell me that your visit here is justified. Just keep away from Sadie and get the hell back to Tamura before I break your neck.'

There was the sound of footsteps and Serena padded swiftly across the room to peer through the window. Bren was standing there smoking a cigarette and watching Kerry walk away. He stood high and wide-shouldered with the beloved arrogance against which Serena was helpless. He was wearing moleskin trousers, well cut, elastic-sided boots and a wide-brimmed hat. He was a grazier from the outback far removed from the world of Serena Downs. And he loved Sadie MacNeith.

Turning from the window, Serena noticed the two blankets spread across the coverlet on the bed. They had not been there last night when she had slipped into bed, but she did recall wakening in the night aware of being cold and in the same moment felt something warm keeping the cold out. It had been almost as though someone was tucking her up, and she wondered who it could have been. Probably Julia.

The next moment she had forgotten all about it and had taken a shower to begin the circulation again after popping out of a warm bed into the cool morning air. She was dressing when Julia came in, surprised and pleased to see her up.

She gave the impression of having been up for hours herself. 'Not staying in bed until the morning warms up, I see. Had a good night?' She looked at the extra blankets on the bed, and added, 'So you put on more blankets. Sensible girl. It does tend to go very cold in the night.'

Serena was fastening the waist of her moleskin trousers and Julia eyed them with approval, noting the trim waist and firm pointed bust shaping the shirt blouse top in fine jersey wool.

Baldly she asked, 'Are you just dressing up, or do you ride?'

Serena laughed. 'I ride, have done from a very early age. Mother had a riding school.'

'That's nice. You look very sweet and sophisticated in that outfit. Known Bren long?'

Julia's voice was too casual and did not deceive Serena one bit as the older woman sat down in a chair near to the window and crossed jodhpur-clad legs.

Guardedly she said, 'I've been in Sydney for some months. Why?'

Julia shrugged, lifted her head and listened to the sound of galloping hooves and a man's laugh followed by that of a girl. When they had faded away she said, 'There goes my reason for asking—Sadie and Bren. He's riding out to see our neighbour for me and Sadie is going with him. If ever a couple were made for each other they are.'

With a calm that she was far from feeling, Serena combed her hair as Julia went on, 'No doubt you saw plenty of graziers and their wives in Sydney for the Show?'

'Yes, I did. The women were so smart and pretty. As for the men'—Serena laughed again, 'their virility and charm knocked me over quicker than a ten-pin ball! My friend Dee adored them.'

'And you?'

Serena put down the comb and touched her neat hair lightly, flicking the curling ends across her forehead. She said equably,

'You mustn't take that remark seriously. As a matter of fact Dee and I came to explore the country. Men didn't enter into our plans. Then unfortunately Dee had to go home.'

'I see.' Julia studied her nails. 'I suppose you find it very romantic with all the tanned, fit males about. You're right, of course. The shortage of girls makes it pretty certain that any newcomers are soon fêted and made much of. The average Australian male is usually high, wide and handsome and presents a very attractive target to unattached girls. Besides being very masculine he becomes a loving, possessive husband and father. I know, because I married one. The tragedy of it is, he does on occasions choose the wrong kind of wife.'

Very quietly Serena asked, 'And just why are you telling me this?'

'Because I like you and I don't want you to get hurt.'

Serena assumed a coolness she was far from feeling and was resolved not to show it. Her smile was tolerant, the question lightly put.

'Why should I get hurt?'

'As you can't know much about our country yet, I'll tell you. During the Show in Sydney lots of girls fraternise with the graziers. It's a great thing to marry a grazier since most of them are established and own large stations. Unfortunately most of the city girls are out for what they can get. All they think about is parties, holidays abroad, going to town to buy pretty things and entertaining to show them off. Everything has to be on a lavish scale, with their pictures in the magazines at some important function or other.'

Serena said quietly, 'Even so some of them must fall in love sometimes, and a grazier might have all the appearance of a Greek god, but he's only a man after all. Wouldn't you agree?'

Julia did not smile. She said soberly, 'Sadie is my daughter by adoption, and it's my dearest wish to see her married to Bren. At the moment she doesn't seem to know what she wants, but she'll come round to my way of thinking in the end.' Julia smiled now as if there was no doubt about it. 'Did you have many dates in Sydney? But of course you must have done, a pretty girl like you.'

Serena said guilelessly, 'I liked Sydney very much. It's a fabulous city and everyone was so friendly.'

'I'm sure they were.' Julia's remark was without rancour and she rose to her feet. 'Shall we go in to breakfast?'

In the huge kitchen with its up-to-date cookers, well equipped cupboards and other amenities, a long table was laid for breakfast. They were met by the pleasing aroma of freshly baked bread, and the savoury aroma of cooked meats and freshly made coffee. Madris, the cook, a stocky little man, was clearing the table of left-overs from early breakfasters.

Julia said, 'Try the pawpaw, Serena. You'll enjoy it if you like fruit.'

After breakfast Julia escorted Serena around the homestead, and the awkwardness brought on by the older woman's questions earlier on was soon forgotten in her interest in the place. There were eight bedrooms, four bathrooms, spacious lounges, larders, storerooms and offices. At the back were well laid out gardens, and tennis courts. Beyond lay the paddocks.

Gazing across them, Serena thought of Bren riding somewhere out there with Sadie. There was a possibility of their making it up, in which case she would be free to go. Serena was not sure which upset her the most, the fact that Bren was out with Sadie or the thought of leaving him for ever.

Meanwhile Julia was suggesting that they ride out to the polo grounds, a matter of two miles away. To Serena's sensitive perception her hostess was obviously going to put her to the test to see if she could really ride. The woman was a dynamo of energy of the kind who had washed, ironed, cleaned, cooked, sewed, her way through marriage besides finding time to help at the station. Her surprise at Serena's ability not only to sit on a horse but also to look good on it was gratifying, although Julia's obsession to have Bren marry Sadie left little room for praise of a prospective rival. Serena patted the satiny neck of her horse and rode off with Julia across the paddocks.

Julia was saying, 'We put on a game of polo every Saturday in which we all join by taking a picnic lunch. The village is only a few miles away from the playing fields, so we have a fair amount of people joining in.'

The polo field had a pavilion at one end and permanent trestle tables set out in the open beneath an iron roof open on two sides. Here the spectators and players gathered after the game to eat, drink and discuss the day's play. Julia was explaining all this to Serena when three riders came into view, Bren, Sadie and another man, well set up and good-looking, with a small neat moustache.

She felt the man's eyes as she sat slim as a willow with a grace demanding attention and completely in harmony with the movements of her pony. A look of dawning admiration filled his narrowed gaze as he took in the colouring and bloom of her youthful cheeks. Her well groomed appearance seemed part of herself, natural and feminine; also she was sensitive and intelligent, he thought, a darn good choice on Bren's part. While he could not imagine her on Tamura, contending with the problems of refractory employees, sick animals, and the loneliness of being a grazier's wife along with the endless unpleasant duties it entailed, she had grit.

Julia said, 'Serena, this is Walt Field, my manager. Walt, meet Serena Downs.'

'Delighted to meet you,' he said. 'The bush wires have been buzzing like mad with the news of Bren's arrival with his girl-friend. You sit a horse well, ma'am. Done much riding?'

Serena, taken aback by his candid approach and now a little embarrassed by his blatant admiration, blinked. 'A little,' she admitted.

'Some are born to the saddle,' he went on with a grin. 'I'd say you were, ma'am.'

A dead silence followed this last remark during which Julia's and Sadie's expressions of disapproval were almost tangible. As for Bren, he sat like a statue carved in bronze, eagle-eyed and unsmiling.

It was Julia who broke the tension. 'You've made a conquest there, Serena. I can see that Sadie will have to look to her laurels.'

It was kindly said, but the words stung nevertheless. Serena hoped that the embarrassed colour mantling her cheeks would go unnoticed, at least by Bren. She felt herself at a disadvantage, but refused to make the usual coy rejoinder that the man Walt would expect.

Then Bren was riding forward to join her and Julia. Keeping in between them as they turned back for the Cockatoo, he said lazily to his aunt,

'I've been told you're thinking of buying part of Platt's land. Haven't you enough to contend with as it is without extending your boundaries?'

Julia's manner was deceptively light. 'I like the idea of enlarging the Cockatoo. Wouldn't like to come in with me, would you?'

Her tone was low with the intention of not letting Walt

or Sadie hear as they followed them leisurely.

Bren, however, had no such qualms. 'I would not. By the way, I've been talking to Platt and will give you all the details when we get back.'

His answer to Julia's offer was curt and to the point. Whatever his aunt had let him in for it was evidently something that he was determined not to become involved in. For the rest of the way they continued to discuss market prices for their stock, and Bren compared advantages with disadvantages of things he had seen at the Agricultural Show.

From time to time he cast a mocking glance at Serena riding beside him. Her face was fresh and vividly alive and his eyes lingered to meet the steady regard of her deep blue ones between their long curling lashes.

'Enjoying your ride?' he asked when conversation slackened off as they reached the homestead.

'Very much. No need to ask if you have,' she replied.

Julia had gone on ahead and for a moment Sadie and Walt had not caught up with them as they dismounted.

'And just what is that supposed to mean?' he queried on an uplifted brow.

Serena smiled at him sweetly and swung herself down from her horse.

'Like old times, was it? Riding with Sadie, I mean.'

His eyes narrowed down at her. 'That kind of remark asks for reprisals,' he murmured.

'Strange, I thought Sadie was the one asking for reprisals,' she answered, and followed Julia to the house.

After lunch Bren suggested taking Serena out to the stables to see a newly born foal.

'What kind of a riding stable had your mother?' he asked conversationally as he strolled beside her to the stables.

'Not a big one. Ten horses and around half a dozen small ponies for the younger ones.'

'What happened?'

'She died.'

He had pushed his hands into his pockets and was looking down at her tolerantly. The streaky blonde hair framing the pure lines of her face caught and held beams from the sun. She walked beside him as light as thistledown, and seemingly way out of his reach.

'And your father?' he probed.

'He died, too.'

A moment or so went by, then he said, 'Why didn't you take over the riding school and run it yourself?'

Suddenly he met the barrage of dark blue eyes. 'I wasn't old enough,' she vouchsafed frankly. 'I went to live with Dee's mother. She was Mother's best friend.'

By the time they reached the stables the mother recently relieved of her offspring had her head down and was licking it gently. The colt had not as yet unfolded his spindly legs and the mother was crooning softly in answer to his weak whinnies.

Moving forward, Serena unconsciously gripped Bren's arm, her dark blue eyes shone up into his for a second before more cautious movements brought her near enough to see the newly born colt stagger uncertainly to its feet.

'Isn't it delicious?' she whispered, her eyes glowing in wondrous excitement as the colt tottered forward to muzzle up against its mother.

In the silence that followed Serena gave a deep sigh of pure pleasure and in doing so encountered Bren's gaze fixed upon her. The silence stretched into eternity as she was unable to drag her gaze away from his.

'Hi, there!' Sadie strolled up to them tongue in cheek. 'How goes it? Ah, a newcomer already? Well done, Moonbeam!'

She patted the satiny neck as it bent in loving admiration of its offspring. Her reaction to the colt was in marked contrast to Serena's wide-eyed ecstasy, and she turned to regard her coolly.

'We could call him Sereno. After all, it will be something to remember you by when you've gone.'

Sadie was looking at her with a quiet indifferent smile

and Serena was not caught off guard. She was becoming used to tackling the unexpected and she was aware that Sadie was letting her know that her visit to the Cockatoo would not be so very important since it would not be of long duration. Also a woman who had known Bren for so long would not easily let him go. Goodness, she thought, I'm the other woman where Sadie is concerned! Her hand had dropped from Bren's arm at the other girl's approach and he drawled lazily:

'Why not call it Star? See the small white mark on its forehead?'

He was looking at Sadie narrow-eyed and mocking, and Serena felt herself forgotten as the other two shared a glance. His words were like a douche of cold water shutting her out still further. So stunned was she that the track of conversation was lost for at least two minutes. When she recovered Sadie was speaking.

'As usual you're right, Bren,' she conceded. Then she began looking down closer at the small white mark on the colt's forehead. 'It is a star. How clever of you!'

'Do you mean the colt or Bren?' Serena said to cover her hurt.

Sadie looked provocatively at Bren, then turned a smiling mouth and unsmiling eyes to Serena's face.

'The colt, of course,' she replied. 'Actually I came to ask you if you'd care for a game of tennis this afternoon. It's quite cool under the trees and I can lend you a racquet if you play.'

Serena had had more than enough of Bren for the time being and she grabbed at the chance of leaving him.

'I'd be glad to play. But I'm a bit rusty as regards practice.'

'That's all right.'

Sadie linked arms with them both and strolled between them to the homestead.

'Incidentally, Mother wants to see you in her office, Bren. Something about business, she said.'

It took all Serena's powers of concentration to play a

good game of tennis that afternoon. Besides being out of practice she was still staggering over Bren's dismissal of Sadie's suggestion of her name for the colt. Why had he done it? The only explanation was that he did not intend to have anything to remind him of her when she had gone. Could it be that he had a thing about the English coming to his country? The idea was feasible, yet she would have sworn that Bren was above such petty thinking.

In such a mood it was not surprising that Sadie won the match hands down. Her victory seemed to mollify the girl, who linked her arm in a friendly way from the court.

'Don't you mind being beaten?' she asked when later they were lying stretched out on loungers on the verandah sipping iced drinks.

Serena closed her eyes on a feeling of homesickness. 'It isn't a matter of whether you win or not, is it? Rather a matter of playing the game in the right way, wouldn't you say?'

Sadie stretched out long golden limbs beneath white shorts. 'I hate to lose. I'm just not built that way. I simply refuse to be beaten at anything—and I mean anything, no holds barred.'

Her tone was so vehement that Serena opened her eyes to look at her in surprise. Was there a threat in the words? Here, she thought, is the woman Bren should have married, the woman who loves him in her fashion, the wife he wants. She swallowed the cold drink with the feeling that at her first sign of weakness Sadie would be right there to conquer.

The hours of daylight were going like a breeze with everything that was strange and new colouring her day. Serena was thankful for the respite away from Bren, but it did not prevent her from thinking about him constantly as he remained with his aunt in her office. What Julia had told her about a grazier marrying one of his own kind remained uppermost in her mind. There was no doubt about it, Julia was a tough cookie, so was Sadie. Were they the kind of women graziers preferred, with no falling in love as a prelude to marriage? After all, it was said that the weaker sex were the tougher in the long run. But Serena could never see herself as a second Julia or Sadie.

Maybe the country had something to do with it, kind of toughening one up. However, where Bren was concerned, Serena could never be tough. Indeed, she was discovering that her love for him had made her hypersensitive where he was concerned.

CHAPTER FIVE

SERENA dressed for the barbecue that evening with warm clothing in mind. Her wardrobe was limited, but fortunately she had an overdress in fine tweed cut on model lines beneath which she could wear a smart shirt. A white woolly jacket draped around her shoulders would keep out the cold and could be discarded when necessary.

It occurred to her as she dressed that she would see Bren in action for the first time among his relatives and friends. That careless charm would be very much in evidence along with his endearing grin, and it would be as well to prepare herself for his interest in Sadie. She sighed. Life was never as one pictured it. There were so many snags and pitfalls to be aware of. One was her caring too deeply for Bren. She was in danger of becoming too emotional where he was concerned, and her best plan would be to play it cool.

The guests had been arriving for some time and her nervousness increased at the sound of car doors slamming, accompanied by jolly voices and light laughter. At last, assuming a false calm, she lightly flicked a curl into place, draped the white woolly jacket around her shoulders and opened the french window of her room leading out on to the verandah. The idea was for her to go out that way in order to see the guests arrive and so prepare herself for meeting a crowd of strangers who, because she was Bren's friend, would show a lively interest in herself. As she stepped outside a tall figure straightened from the wall.

'Good evening.' Bren smiled down at her and her heart lurched. Her eyes were deep blue pools in a delicately flushed face as she struggled for a certain degree of calm. He was not to know that her heart was beating abnormally

as he towered above her. The wide shoulders in the tweed
jacket seemed to take on wider dimensions as he grinned
down at her and shook his head in mock dismay.

'Sticks out a mile that you're a city girl,' he drawled.
'You'd look sophisticated in an old sack. You smell nice
too.' He bent his head to breathe in the fragrance of her
hair. 'Hmm. . . .' he ended. 'Good enough to eat!'

Serena laughed and moved back a step, finding his nearness more than unsettling. 'I hope it isn't that kind of barbecue! I'm scared enough as it is, meeting all your friends
and relations.'

'Nothing to be scared of, unless it's the males. They'll
probably swarm around you like bees around a honey-
pot. When that happens just remember that you're supposed to be my girl.' His voice had dropped to an omin-
ously low pitch and he took her slim shoulders between
strong hands. 'Maybe I ought to have bought you a ring.'

'A ring?' she echoed with a catch at her heart. 'Isn't that
taking things a bit too far?'

'Hi there!'

Sadie's voice hit the air like a warning bell. Serena
moved out of Bren's strong grip and his hands dropped, as
Sadie moved forward in a beautifully embroidered black
evening skirt and matching poncho.

Bren's eyebrows lifted and he shared his grin between
them. 'You two certainly add something to the landscape.
Pity you can't cook as well as you look.'

Sadie said acidly, 'That's what I like about you men. You
want the best of both worlds. What is it you want, Bren?
A presentable wife or a Cordon Bleu cook?'

'Both,' he grinned, and instantly they were surrounded
by guests who were mounting the verandah steps.

In the midst of laughter and pleasantries Serena was introduced to people as informal as the dress they wore.
Some were distant relatives of Bren who regarded her with
friendly curiosity, and everyone appeared delighted upon
seeing a fresh face. Soon she was surrounded and bom-
barded with questions, food and drink. The steaks and

chops freshly barbecued were delicious and she munched
happily along with the rest asking endless questions herself about life in the outback and the way of life there.
Bush yarns soon became the order of the day, and she
was sure that no one could tell a tall story like a true
Aussie. The expert way in which they were told made it
impossible for anyone as naïve as herself to decide if the
stories were genuine or merely leg-pulls. The cries of derision arising from time to time from the listeners, though,
made her doubt the authenticity of any of them. Nevertheless, she enjoyed them all immensely and wiped tears of
mirth from her dancing eyes in a way that seemed to draw
Bren's gaze her way.

They were all sitting on anything handy—chairs, tables,
tree stumps, all within the glow of the fire. Serena was surrounded by young men encouraged there by the clever
manoeuvring of Julia earlier on. The young men had fallen
in with her plans enthusiastically. It was not often that the
chance came their way of meeting a young woman from
another country whose charm and prettiness were in complete harmony with the rest of her.

Bren, Serena noticed, was moving indolently among the
guests after being hauled in to help his aunt and Sadie dis-
tribute the food and drink. Madris, the Cockatoo's chef,
was in charge of the barbecue and Sadie was grasping the
opportunity to be with Bren. She was never far away from
his elbow, a fact that made Serena wonder if it was a ruse
on Julia's part to bring the two together. The woman was
tenacious, and Serena shrank inwardly at the way she
flaunted her ambitions for her daughter.

To Serena's sensitive perception it was rather humiliat-
ing for a girl to be flung at a man's head unless that man
was willing. Also that the girl was sure of him. But was
she? Was that why she had played him up? Certainly
Bren seemed to enjoy her companionship as he laughed
with her at remarks made by the guests as they moved
among them.

Serena was laughing merrily over a tall story when Bren

pushed his way through the guests around her. He said on
an air of command,

'Come on, boys, break it up. Go and hog someone else's
girl!'

Up to now there had been more eating than drinking,
so everyone was replete from a surfeit of good food and
pleasant companionship, and there was good-natured bantering from the men, who moved away without any fuss.
During the absorbing and interesting conversation with the
boys around her Serena had, for the moment, forgotten
Bren. Now she realised that a band of brawny Aussies
were no match for him when he wanted to clear the decks,
as it were. Come to think of it, he didn't look in too good
a humour either. Was he regretting bringing her with him?
For a moment he towered above her, his face a bronze cast
in the flickering light. His eyes looked almost black.

'You're proving quite an attraction, Serena.' He dropped
down beside her to fling a careless arm around her
shoulders. 'Surprising how one little English chick can
bowl over so many Aussie wolves.'

But not you, she was tempted to say. It was all so carelessly done, the encircling arm, the deep mocking drawl
that she had to steady her racing pulses and accept the
situation as naturally as he did.

Madris, having finished the cooking, was passing drinks
around, and someone started to sing to the twang of a
guitar. Bren had a pleasing baritone voice which he used
to good effect and time passed pleasantly. When someone
threw fresh logs on the dying fire Serena quivered unconsciously, and instantly Bren picked up the white woolly
jacket she had discarded earlier to help her into it.

In that moment she caught the glare of Sadie's eyes
across the spurting glow of the fire. It was venomous. The
next moment Sadie was tossing down the rest of her drink.
Feeling rather guilty that the girl had mistaken Bren's protective action, Serena was about to ask him to invite Sadie
over to them. Then she remembered her reason for being
there. He would not thank her for interfering. He had, no

doubt, laid plans of his own to that end and if he was
teaching Sadie a lesson it was up to him to make the first
move. Even so, she hated to see Sadie was drinking far
more than was good for her. Drinks were being handed
around with monotonous precision as someone suggested
drinking a toast to the polo players taking part in Saturday's match. Toasts were drunk to Julia and then Bren; then
someone suggested a toast to his girl-friend Serena.

Serena was sitting with Bren on the sawn off base of a
massive tree a little apart from the crowd on a small rise.
Instantly all heads were turned in their direction and she
felt her face go hot beneath the sea of eyes. Suddenly a
swaying figure came stumbling towards them holding her
glass aloft.

'Here's to Sh-Sh-Sherena.' Sadie's words were slurred
with drink as she swayed in front of them. 'Don't look so
embarrassed, Sherena. We're all your friends, even if your
ways are ... shall I shay ... more advanced than ours.'
Sadie began to giggle helplessly, wobbled perilously,
seemed about to fall, then swung round to face the gleam
of upturned faces. 'Looksh as if butter wouldn't melt in her
mouth, doeshn't she, folks? Well, I'll let you into a little
... a very little shecret.' The slurred tones sank down to
a stage whisper as she miraculously kept her balance and
bent forward. 'I saw Bren leaving Sherena's bedroom long
after everybody had gone to bed lasht night. What do you
think of that? One way to get your man!'

Sadie straightened after delivering her bombshell and
attempted to finish the remainder of her drink after spill-
ing most of it. She was watched in complete silence.
Serena's face was ashen. Her hands were clenched and her
nails dug into her palms as Bren's arm contracted around
her. The man with the guitar began to strum the tune
'Jealousy' and someone said,

'Pipe down, Sadie. You're drunk.'

Bren's voice was as lazy and unconcerned as ever. He
spoke almost as though he had expected Sadie's outburst.

'And why not?' he demanded of her. 'I had every right to be in Serena's room.'

Sadie turned and drew herself up to eye him defiantly. 'With her permission, no doubt,' she cried insolently.

'That's right,' Bren countered coolly. 'Folks, allow me to present the future mistress of Tamura.'

There was another second or so of deadly silence, then the roar went up. The shouts were deafening. Remarks like, 'You sly dog!' and 'You lucky so-and-so!' rent the air. Someone called, 'A toast to Bren and Serena!' and everybody drank. All, that was, except Bren and Serena, who had risen on shaking legs ready to flee. But Bren stood like a rock at her side, his grasp of her tightening.

'Sadie,' he commanded in a deep throaty growl, 'you will apologise to Serena immediately.'

Sadie threw her glass down viciously in front of them and it smashed to pieces. 'So you're married,' she jeered. 'Why didn't you say so instead of holding out on us? How long did you say you'd been in Sydney, Serena? Two months? Quick wedding, was it?'

Serena quivered and tried to break free from Bren's hold, but it was a futile effort against his strength. Julia had now moved to join them, looking strained and tense.

'You must excuse Sadie, Bren,' she said, taking hold of her daughter's arm. 'She's drunk and doesn't know what she's saying.'

Bren said harshly, in dangerous tones, 'She knows what she's saying all right. Her voice just now was perfectly controlled, and an apology is called for. She has insulted a guest in your house, the rest is up to her. If an apology is not forthcoming then this is the last time we shall set foot in the Cockatoo.'

His voice, like Julia's, was low and meant for their ears alone. The guests were now talking together amiably, giving the impression that this was not the first time someone had taken a drink too many and created a scene. It happened all the time when people got together and let their hair down. Serena was uneasily surmising all this as she looked up at Bren's set jaw. He was furious all right, but for what reason? There was no doubt in her mind now that he was the one who had entered her bedroom to put the extra blankets on her bed in case she had been cold and had not been told where the extra ones were kept. Was he angry because Sadie had seen him leaving her room and so made it impossible for any reconciliation to take place now between them? Serena wished she knew.

As it was, Sadie had her sympathy. If Bren had hoped to teach the girl a lesson then he had certainly done so. She was obviously in love with him. Serena felt sick of the whole business and longed to end it. She caught Bren's arm. 'Let Sadie go indoors. There's no need for her to apologise to me. I'll go myself too.'

Bren said quietly, 'We're waiting, Sadie.'

Julia was saying impatiently to her daughter, 'For heaven's sake apologise! I don't know what's got into you, making an exhibition of yourself like this!'

Sadie began to look sick and she turned to mumble something to Bren and Serena before fleeing into the house.

Bren did not watch her go. But as she disappeared into the gloom he addressed all the guests.

'Thanks for your good wishes, folks. I didn't mean to keep you in the dark for long, but it isn't my intention to do you out of a wedding party.' Here his charming smile lifted the corners of his mouth. 'I thought a celebration at Tamura would be more the thing after I've carried my bride over the threshold.'

Listening to him and watching him win over the guests with his own special brand of charm, Serena thought numbly how cleverly he had handled a sticky situation. He had told no lies, had not openly admitted to marrying her, yet he had implied exactly that in his lazy nonchalant fashion. Bitterly, she knew that he would be just as clever in breaking off the so-called marriage with herself when the time came. Unlike Sadie and a few of the others, he had not drunk a lot—she would say that for him. In fact she had seen him take only one drink after the barbecue.

But it brought cold comfort to her aching heart to dwell upon his sterling qualities.

Julia had followed Sadie indoors and the barbecue went on as if nothing had happened. Bren caught Serena's arm after his little speech to the guests and said urgently, 'We have to talk.'

He propelled her away from the merrymaking to a quieter side of the homestead where earlier they had gone to see the newborn foal. As the sounds they had left became muted Serena tried to absorb a little of the quiet serenity and failed miserably. Bren's fingers around her elbow were sending all kinds of vibrations through her. The thought that he had been responsible for the extra blankets on her bed the previous night gave her the feeling that life had a few redeeming features after all.

Bren was watching the pale enchantment of her face when she lifted a gaze that hungered with a sweet smile. Vainly she fought against his magnetism, finding it as wonderful as when they were at the Show in Sydney and heaven had been very near. Disconcerted, she raised a hand to her face, felt it burning hot and spoke quickly to cover her embarrassment.

'So it was you who came into my room to put extra blankets on the bed?'

Bren shoved his hands into his pockets. His dark intent face hardened a little.

'That's right. Newcomers to this country don't realise how the temperature can drop at night.' He paused, then continued as if he felt that further explanations were called for. 'I wasn't sure whether you'd been told about the extra bed linen in the cupboards of your room.'

She said wistfully and inconsequently, 'No harm was done, except of course to our reputation if the truth was known.'

Slowly they began to walk across a paddock in the cool summer night. The bright stars in the cold sky were no more chilled than her heart. They were side by side, bound in a strange dark unity, yet kept apart by outward forces which defeated her.

Bren said forcefully, 'Before we begin to discuss important issues I may as well tell you that Sadie's exhibition earlier on is only one of many. It isn't the first time she's been inebriated, nor will it be the last. The merest trifles set her off, like taking the mickey out of her mother or livening up what she sees as a dull party. If she can't hog anything else at the time she hogs the limelight by getting drunk.'

Serena's voice hung on the night air in a tiny clear whisper.

'I wouldn't say that what happened to her this evening was a mere trifle. She was shattered at your announcement that I was going to be your future partner at Tamura. I don't think you could have put it in a more hurtful way.'

He said harshly, 'You have to remember that I have to pit my wits against those of two designing women. I rather gathered that you would have the impression that neither Sadie nor my aunt Julia were exactly delighted with my announcement. The thing is that we're in this too deep now to wriggle out at the drop of a hat. We have to do something about it.'

'What do you suggest?'

Her whisper reached him as he stepped towards the paddock fence where he leaned his back against it to face her. Serena moved by his side, reaching out to the fence as though grasping at a lifeline. For palpitating moments Bren glanced down at the pale velvet sheen of her skin, the dark-lashed depths of her eyes, the gleam of her hair.

He said slowly, 'I think a temporary marriage is called for.'

'You . . . you do?'

Serena's stomach lurched and her heart beat suffocatingly fast. Further words were beyond her for the moment.

He smiled lazily. 'Don't look so stricken! It won't go beyond the bounds of the actual ceremony.'

The telltale heat came into her face, but her voice was steady.

'Don't you think you're being a bit drastic? Most of the people drinking back there will have forgotten most of what happened this evening when they've sobered up tomorrow. Besides, your aunt Julia isn't likely to allow a little ... er ... indiscretion on your part, like being seen coming from my room, to come between you and Sadie.'

He let a minute elapse. Then coolly, 'Aren't you forgetting that I gave the impression just now that you and I were already married? As an eligible bachelor I've been the target for matchmaking mums around, including my aunt, for years. Besides, I'm touchy when it comes to my friends and relations making conjectures about you and me. Also,' sardonically, 'I don't happen to be drunk. I'm cold sober.'

Inadequately she said, 'I suppose it is a solution to the problem.'

Her voice had wobbled towards the end of the sentence, and after a silence, he remarked a little roughly, 'I wish you wouldn't look as if I'm suggesting something positively indecent. I happen to see things your way as well as my own. It hasn't occurred to you, has it, that your tour of the country as my wife will be under ideal conditions. You'll have my protection and no qualms as regards stopping-off places. Furthermore, what better guide could you have than an Aussie who lives here?'

Serena wished that her jumbled and distorted thoughts were as clear and cool as the night air. She saw herself as a pliable lovesick girl so much under the spell of her beloved that she was like soft putty in his hands. She had a frightening sensation of being grabbed by the hand of fate and pulled roughly along to a situation that would combine both pain and ecstasy, pain because their marriage would be a fiasco, ecstasy because Bren would belong to her by law through a marriage of convenience.

With a tiny quivering smile which had she but known it made her look quite beautiful, she said, 'Sounds feasible, but really I didn't mind going around on my own, and the uncertainty was part of the adventure, part of the fun of discovering things.'

His features suddenly hardened. 'It's not a good idea for a young woman to go around on her own these days. On the other hand, you can continue making your own way afterwards. The marriage between us is something we can dispose of later.' He softened and laid a hand over the one nearest to him on the fence. 'Believe me, it's the best way. Even now wedding presents could be on their way to Tamura. I bet the air is thick with the news that Bren Robart has been caught hook, line and sinker by an English miss.'

Standing there with his hand covering her own, Serena felt his warm vitality seeping through her numbed senses. Plucking up enough courage to look him in the face, she said with difficulty, 'How do you propose we get married without anybody knowing about it?'

'Quite easily. My lawyer Dill Harris has left Sydney on a visit to his father up north. I propose to tell Julia that we're going there to make arrangements for a marriage settlement for you. It will be true in a way, because Dill's father happens to be a retired clergyman who can perform the wedding ceremony for us. I shall telephone Dill right away to tell him we're coming in a matter of hours and that he's to have the necessary ring sent from Sydney by special delivery for when we arrive.'

'But won't that be very expensive for you? I—I mean, having rings flown out for me to choose my size and the special licence? Won't that be a problem too?'

'Dill has special correspondence sent out concerning his work while he stays with his parents, so he'll be able to manage it all right. I can also trust them to say nothing about the actual ceremony. Furthermore,' Bren's voice was humorous, 'you need have no worry about the ceremony being valid since it will go no farther than signing the necessary papers. Now I want you to go and have a good sleep, since we shall be starting out early in the morning.'

'How early?'

'Half past six. You can catch up on your sleep in the car.'

As he spoke Serena could hear cars leaving the station and goodbyes being called as the guests departed. She quivered a little, realising it was after midnight. The moon was as bright as day and amid the cool nocturnal scents both strange and chilling, there was no sweet intimacy between them as they walked back to the homestead. Bren's arm was draped across her slim shoulders and a faint air of malice directed itself to her from him.

'At least the party broke up on a note of surprise. It will do Aunt Julia good not to have her own way for once in a while. I like my aunt, I'm very fond of her, but I don't like bossy women. They're out of place.'

Serena said demurely, 'Are you aiming at putting her in her place too?'

He grinned. 'Not really. What Aunt Julia does is her own business, as long as that business doesn't overlap mine.'

Serena said, 'I can't help being curious about why you refused to go in with her on that business deal she offered. Surely if you're not very well off it would be to your advantage to accept her offer?'

'I go into no partnership with any woman,' he replied flatly. 'I do my own thing in my own way.' Suddenly he frowned. 'Why this questioning? Just because we're getting married it doesn't give you any different status from what you have now, other than to outward appearances.'

Serena smiled impishly. 'I'm only reacting in the way you implied I would be enjoying the protection of a husband. Who knows? I might even start bossing you around a bit when we're married to give a little more reality to the whole show.'

His face darkened. 'I shouldn't advise that if I were you. That's what I would call living dangerously.'

She looked up into the gleam in his eyes and with her pulses racing murmured,

'According to you I was living dangerously when you caught up with me.'

'Ah, but soon the situation between us will be slightly

different. For instance, if you should then begin to take the mickey out of me, I might retaliate in a way you won't like. Far better leave things to me, little partner. That way you won't be hurt.'

Serena swallowed on a dry throat. 'How do I know I can trust you?' she demanded. 'I can change my mind about marrying you.'

'You don't and you won't,' he answered laconically. 'Afraid, are you? Then it's a challenge for you, or are you all talk about liking adventure?'

They had reached the verandah of the homestead and he bunched a strong brown fist to place it beneath her chin in a playful feint. For a moment Serena gazed up at him wide-eyed and palpitating. Then without another word she turned and fled to her room, closing the french window behind her with a bang. Bren's deep chuckle followed her.

What kind of an idiot was she, to place all her trust in a big uncaring man from the outback who had no time for women in his world? If she had not been so sunk about him she would be taking the part of Julia and Sadie. Serena undressed with her loyalties torn to shreds. Viewing the situation impersonally, Bren was really in need of help. But like all men he would not admit it. Instead he was covering up his need by pretending that she needed his protection instead of vice versa. She needed protection all right, but it was from the man himself. It didn't make sense. But then neither did her love for him.

Sleep was a long time in coming and she was awake again at five o'clock. Rising early would give her time for a luxuriously warm bath. But her head was heavy, her limbs lethargic as she began to dress. Her wardrobe was limited, but the tailored sleeveless dress in soft oatmeal jersey that always came up so beautifully when washed was ideal with its matching coat.

Since leaving her bed Serena had kept her mind empty of thought. Now that she was ready all those disturbing thoughts came back in full force. The forthcoming ceremony and all it entailed filled her with qualms. She would have to be very careful since they were playing a game. She was frightened, but she was also confident. The thing was to be strong enough to handle this affair.

The peremptory tap on her door could only be Bren's, and he came in with her early morning drink. He was wearing the tweed jacket and his city-going trousers, and he closed her door behind him to survey her with a grin.

'That's what I like about you,' he said. 'You don't keep a fellow waiting.' His eagle eyes took in her slender figure in the sleeveless dress. Under the blonde streaky hair her deep blue eyes emphasised the delicate cut of her features. Her cheeks had the colouring of peach blossom, her chin and throat were enchantingly shaped. A look of wondering admiration came into his eyes, then he gave her the drink and leaned back against the door as she accepted it.

'How are you feeling?' he asked.

'I have the bride's usual symptoms,' she replied. 'A thick head and I don't want any breakfast.'

He watched with a slight frown as she drank from the cup, then he said,

'Your head will clear after a sleep in the car during the journey. As for breakfast, Madris is filling a flask and making up some food for us.' He paused and looked meaningfully at the faint shadows under her eyes. 'Worried about something, or doesn't getting up early in the mornings agree with you?'

Serena finished the rest of her drink thirstily, and lifted a militant chin to say primly, 'Rising early has never been one of my problems. I hate staying in bed, but as this is the first time for me to get married naturally I have qualms, even if it's only to be a temporary affair.'

Straightening indolently from the door, he took the empty cup from her and placed it down on the bedside table. 'As this also happens to be the first time for me that makes two of us. I told you there was nothing to worry about.' His eyes darkened in colour as they searched her face, and gradually his mouth lifted humorously at the corners. 'However, I must confess that it's heartening to know, as a prospective bridegroom, that my future bride won't need kicking out of bed in the mornings.'

Serena met his grin with a look of disdain. 'Very funny!'

'To a grazier I'd say it was very important,' he contradicted.

She said grimly, 'You know something? I'm glad I'm not marrying you for real. You don't need a woman, you need a pint-size man, not born but blasted from rock. I think you'll make a pretty awful husband.'

'Spoken like a true Brit,' he drawled, and his chuckle made her long to hit him. 'Time was when a grazier picked a wife by the way she handled a bag of mealies.'

Before Serena could reply to his outrageous statement, he was reaching out for her coat laid ready on her bed, and helping her into it.

'Ready?' he asked, taking her arm as she picked up her handbag and gloves.

He seemed impatient to be gone, striding silently beside her to where his Land-Rover awaited and handing her into the front seat. There was no one about and Serena guessed that Sadie could be sleeping off the effects of her drinking. About Julia she was not sure. Watching Bren covertly as he set the car off at speed, she decided to ask him about his aunt's reaction to them leaving the Cockatoo so suddenly for a day out. But not at the moment, for Bren had drawn into himself. He looked stern, silent and very much the strong man. He also appeared to be travelling at an excessive speed, so much so that he would probably only answer her questions in monosyllables. In the end she closed her eyes and slept.

She opened them again to find the sun had grown in strength and the car was like an oven. She slipped out of her coat as Bren drew up at the side of the road where bottle trees, more grotesque than beautiful, gave little or no shade. Seas of grassland stretched out far into an horizon of distant peaks against an immense blue sky.

'Headache gone?' he enquired as he reached over lazily to the back seat of the car for a picnic box.

She nodded and watched as he withdrew a flask and uncorked it. She said,

'That story just now about the grazier choosing a wife because of her strength, was it true?'

He passed her a cup of coffee, apparently very much amused by her question, and she longed to pierce his nonchalant ease.

'Really want to know?' he queried, pouring out a second cup for himself.

'Of course.'

He sipped part of his drink, placed the cup down on the floor of the car and offered her a box containing sandwiches and fruit.

'It's true, no kidding,' laconically.

Serena sighed profoundly. 'It doesn't make sense.'

'What doesn't?'

Bren opened up his lunch box, extracted a sandwich and bit into it with strong white teeth.

She was amazed and indignant. 'Why, marrying a woman in such a cold-blooded way. I mean, how on earth could such a marriage last? It's positively barbaric!' Her blue eyes attacked his calm. 'And what did you mean just now about me speaking like a true Brit?'

He said lazily, 'Because you've been brought up to believe that man is noble, honourable and bursting with good intentions. He isn't. Not when he lives out in the wilds with none of the modern amenities. Man is barbaric. He stops at nothing to gain his own ends. He's clever. The woman who swung the bag of mealies would never know why he chose her, and she would be happy serving him and bringing up his children.' Suddenly he grinned. 'Who knows, he might have fallen in love with her for her strength? After all, some women do fall in love with a man's strength, his splendid physique. And haven't women through the ages fallen in love with the biggest scoundrels?'

Serena bit into her sandwich and munched. They ate in silence with the soft rustle of the grass making the only sound across the plains. Bren looked content as though he was enjoying the break. He had thrown his big hat on to the back seat of the car and his thick dark springy hair shone with a life of its own. An aura of freedom seemed to encompass him, adding in some subtle way to his vitality and charm.

Serena felt more alone than if she had been dropped in the centre of the outback. Bren refilled her cup and his own, grinned at her polite acceptance and began on another sandwich.

She said, 'What did your aunt Julia say when you told her that we were going out for the day? Was she surprised?'

'Not really. It isn't the first time I've gone to see Dill at his parents' home while staying at the Cockatoo. By the way, she was upset at putting us in separate rooms.'

Serena went scarlet. She all but choked on her coffee. She stammered, 'But how was she to know ... I m-mean, we aren't ... we weren't ... married.'

He smiled down at her, a mocking smile as he noted her obvious embarrassment, and she looked away.

'We shall be when we get back. That's why I'm telling you.'

'You—you mean. ...' She broke off in dismay and he nodded.

'A married couple do usually occupy the same room. But don't worry, we shall make our own arrangements.'

Her voice shook a little as she said desperately, 'Do we have to go back to the Cockatoo?'

'I'm afraid so. I'm playing polo on Saturday, so they'll expect me to show up.'

He was demolishing another sandwich with an obvious languid indifference to her obvious distress, and she resented his apparent lack of interest in her feelings.

'Don't you think it would be better if you returned to the Cockatoo alone? You could say that I've gone home or something and that I'm coming back later. Then we wouldn't have to go through with a form of marriage.'

The frankness in his eyes gave way to cynicism as he

drawled, 'Got cold feet, have you?'

Anger blazed within her, submerging all fear. 'What do you think? It's you who wants my help. So you ought to think of some solution other than marriage.'

His bantering manner resolved into a fierce tenseness. 'You forget that you agreed to help me in this way, that Dill, my lawyer, is expecting us, that he has the ring probably by now and his father is making all the arrangements for our marriage. Dill is my lifelong friend. We went through college together. What kind of an ass is he going to think me if I arrive without you?'

She stammered, 'But—but girls have let men down before now. . . .'

'But no girl has let Bren Robart down in marriage.' He shrugged. 'If you want to go you're free to leave.'

Serena had never felt so mean in her life. What he said was true. He had also stated time and again that he would play the game by her. Besides, if Sadie's reaction to his so-called marriage was anything to go by it would not be long before things were settled between them. She herself had nothing to lose—only Bren. This was Bren's world and for a short space of time she would be part of it. What did it matter what came after? She would have her memories.

She said quietly, 'I know just how you feel and I do want to help you. I'll do what you say. I want you to be happy.'

He gave her a long look and said mockingly, 'Why this concern over my happiness?'

'Well . . .' she looked at him appealingly, 'I'd like to know that I'd done someone some good by coming here. Besides, by helping you I could be helping myself on my travels. After all, I have to break away some time and continue on my own.'

'We can talk about that later. In the meantime if it's any comfort to you I'm no worse than the next man. I can be the perfect gentleman when I choose,' he told her, his mouth sardonic.

She smiled. 'I believe you. There is one thing, though.'

He raised an attractive brow. 'Yes?' tolerantly.

'I think Sadie cares for you deeply. That's why she drank too much last night. So I'd go easy on her if I were you as regards teaching her a lesson. Maybe she's already learned it.'

Bren was not looking at her. He was gazing forth to the distant hills as if he was seeing things beyond her vision. His brown face was intent, his profile drawn with a ruthless clarity. There was an iron mastery about him that made her quiver inwardly. Then he turned his head slightly in her direction, as if he felt her regard, and their eyes collided, clung.

Serena felt the hot colour warming her face and she lowered her gaze. The pulse quickening in her throat threatened to choke her. He was too near, much too near for her comfort.

His look was faintly whimsical. 'Would you still rather stay here than go back to England?' he said.

Serena did not lift her eyes. 'What do you want to know that for?'

'Because I do.'

'But I thought I told you I was going on where Dee and I left off. I still mean to do just that.'

'Nothing has happened to alter your decision?'

'What could happen?'

He gave a mirthless laugh which she failed to understand, and she replaced the lid on her lunch box. She felt somewhat agitated at his nearness and the intent way with which he regarded her.

He said, 'You aren't very kindly disposed towards me at the moment, are you? What are you afraid of?'

Serena put the lunch box in the container, moved surreptitiously a little further away from him in her seat and lifted her clear eyes to his.

'If you must know, I think you've been rather hard on Sadie.'

He smiled a little. 'Do her good,' he drawled, 'the spoiled brat!'

'Even so it doesn't justify you treating her the way you have,' she persisted.

He put his arm on the wheel of the car and turned to eye her coolly with that irritating intent regard which never failed to move her.

'Sadie has had everything her way since Aunt Julia adopted her as a baby. Pity, otherwise Sadie might have been quite a girl.'

Serena smiled faintly. 'You mean she might have been brought up to handle a heavy bag of mealies?'

Bren laughed. His teeth flashed in his tanned face and her heart lurched.

'You can't forget that, can you?' he scoffed. 'As a matter of fact I like my women very feminine. That doesn't mean that I like them spoilt by a drooling mother giving in to their every whim. Not only does it serve to turn the girl's head, it also makes her self-centred, selfish and intolerant of other people's needs.'

Her voice mocked. 'You appear to know a lot about women.'

He said lazily, 'Much more than you know about men.'

'But then men aren't my favourite subject,' she prevaricated.

'No? I'd say that they were your friend Dee's favourite subject.'

Her blue eyes opened wide. 'That's very clever of you. But I don't happen to be Dee.'

'Pity. I have a feeling I would have found your friend great fun.'

'No doubt Dee would have found you fun too.'

He laughed as though at some secret thought. 'You must give me her address some time. By the way, why have you put your lunch box away before eating the fruit?'

'I enjoyed what I had, thank you.'

He lifted an eyebrow. 'I hope you aren't worrying about anything.'

Serena dusted the skirt of her dress from possible crumbs. Her tone was deliberately light.

'Why should I? You appear to have everything under control.'

He grinned. 'A more experienced woman would find that terribly suspect,' he said.

'Maybe a more experienced woman wouldn't have got so entangled with you,' she retorted.

Bren took an eating apple from his lunch box. 'Have an apple.'

Serena hesitated, aware of him mocking her as he offered it.

'The trouble with you is that you're afraid,' he scoffed.

This time she raised a brow. 'Of an apple?'

'No, of a man.'

She said demurely, 'You can't blame a girl for being careful.'

He looked at her in frank derision. 'Is that what you call it?'

She took the apple and speared him with a look from deep blue eyes.

'There are times,' she replied, 'when I dislike you intensely.'

'And the other times?'

'I prefer an apple.'

CHAPTER SIX

THEY arrived at their destination just before lunch. The sun was well up in the sky and the heat that had surged through Serena's body receded, leaving her with a chill which began around the heart. She looked at Bren, who had been travelling at great speed, and her eyes rested on his strong clear-cut profile, so rigid in its masculinity that it scared her. It was shattering to think that she was travelling to be married to a man who had probably forgotten her presence in the last hour or so.

They had spoken little in the drowsy hot atmosphere, but his next utterance proved that he had been aware of her even though his attention had been given to his driving.

'You'll like the Harris family,' he said equably, swinging the car from the paddocks to a homestead backed by bottle trees and pines. 'They're homely folk and will be tickled pink to see someone from overseas.'

At first glance it was difficult to imagine the elderly man who came out to greet them as being a former member of the church. Deeply tanned with a rugged complexion and piercing blue eyes, he looked like a farmer despite the smart city-going suit he had put on in their honour.

His wife Alma, slim and wiry with fading auburn hair, reminded Serena of Julia except that she had a gentler mien than Bren's indomitable aunt. Her welcome was the free-and-easy one, Australian style, of warmth and pleasure. It was evident that Cliff and Alma Harris were very fond of Bren.

Alma said in mild reproof, 'You don't visit us enough, Bren. And now I suppose you'll soon be off on a honeymoon.'

Bren bent down to kiss her cheek and said easily, 'Not yet. The thing is to get married first.' He slanted a wicked glance down to Serena walking gracefully by his side. 'Serena was on a tour of the country when I persuaded her to marry me. She isn't sure even now that it was a good idea,' he drawled.

Serena was surprised that her feelings showed—but then Bren had an uncanny knack of reading her thoughts. She laughed, was pleased that she was able to do so in the circumstances, and found herself entering more lightheartedly into the affair than she had hoped.

One thing pleased her enormously. Bren was not resorting to any lies to aid and abet their marriage, and this sent her opinion of him soaring. She had decided to say as little as possible herself since her forthright nature would be apt to lead her into tight corners.

A second couple came to greet them in the hall, bringing with them an aura of city life. Dill and Etta Harris were around Bren's age, as far as Serena could judge, around thirty. Dill was inclined to be more dapper than his father and managed to look distinguished in a rural setting.

Etta was dark-eyed and slinky in a suit of fondant green that brought out the green of her eyes. She showed a marked fondness for Bren and a lively curiosity about Serena. Her smile, showing perfect teeth, was warm and friendly as she took Serena's hand.

'You must tell us some time how you managed to land Bren,' she cooed without rancour. 'It's something the matchmaking mothers and their daughters have been trying to do for years without success!'

Bren said goodhumouredly, 'Tut, tut! Stop talking as though I was some kind of elusive fish!'

Etta gazed at him fondly. 'You were just as slippery,' she cooed.

Serena, who had expected the marriage ceremony to be short, was quite unprepared for Cliff Harris's rendering of it. He did not gabble it off, neither did he treat it lightly. He spoke slowly in excellent English as though emphasising and considering every word.

Listening and following his lead, she marvelled at the

maturity and dignity of the people of the outback where there were no inhibitions to cramp their life style as in the cities. Just before the ceremony an elderly man arrived with a selection of rings from a jewellers in Sydney and there were buttonholes for the guests and a spray of flowers for Serena. Dill Harris had certainly seen to things. He and his wife Etta acted as witnesses and the man from the jewellers gave Serena away. Somehow the womenfolk had even found time to ice a fruit cake and pop it into the fridge to harden enough for the wedding luncheon which followed. It was a happy occasion with Cliff enlivening the meal with his droll remarks of wit and wisdom punctuated with long silences in between.

More than once during the meal, with so many beaming faces around her, Serena had felt near to tears at the kindness and easy acceptance shown to a stranger in their midst. When Bren had stood up beside her to cut the cake, which was beautifully decorated with blue lovers' knots, he had looked very masculine and nonchalant with his teeth showing white in his copper-coloured face as he smiled the whole thing along with his special brand of wit and charm.

In her turn she had played the role of the blushing bride, had received the good wishes of them all including the kisses and teasing such ceremonies bring, and had smiled until the muscles of her face ached. But if her face ached her heart ached still more at the thought of deceiving these nice people about their marriage.

But it was done now, and the sensible thing to do was to forget it and enjoy being with Bren for the short length of time they would spend together. The parting would come soon enough. It would help to look upon the next few weeks as precious pearls to be gathered tenderly and stored away in the confines of her memory to brighten the barren days ahead without him. So outwardly she allowed him to take the lead with all the sweet submission of a happy bride. By and by she would discover what he was really like beneath that lazy, careless exterior which he showed to the world and Serena Downs. While she would not be living with him intimately as a wife she would be near enough to learn to know the real man, the owner of a station called Tamura.

Luella, a dark-eyed Aborigine, who was cook and maid in the Harris establishment, was obviously excited and flattered to be waiting on at a wedding reception. She too looked fondly at Bren, and Serena began to wonder what woman didn't. Fortunately for the short time they were there they saw little likelihood of difficult questions being put to them. Bren had intimated that a honeymoon would possibly follow after seeing that everything was right at Tamura. It had surprised Serena that he had not kissed her at the ceremony, and she wondered tremulously whether he was as conscious of the omission as she was. It hurt to think that he had not kissed her, and it went on hurting however often she reminded herself that the marriage was not for real.

Looking back, she was discovering that she had fallen in love with him from their first meeting. Now and only now when it was too late did it occur to her what a fool she had been. Her original intention of going on with her plans despite the absence of her friend Dee had been fine until she had allowed sentimental feelings to outweigh her better sense of judgment.

The urge to repay Bren for giving her a good time at the Show in Sydney by falling in with his plans to teach Sadie a lesson had been wrong. There were dozens of girls he could have chosen from, girls who would have taken a temporary marriage in their stride. He had picked on Serena Downs because she was not worldly-wise and therefore did not present a threat to any future seeking of an annulment to their planned marriage.

So it was that she went with him on the journey back to the Cockatoo with a numbed heart and not a little apprehension. There had been one awkward moment when the wedding presents had been mentioned, but Bren had met it with his usual careless nonchalance.

'Bring them to Tamura when we get back,' he said. 'We'll have a real slap-up do then.'

'Anything particular you'd like, Serena?' asked Etta with a warm friendliness.

Serena, scarlet with guilt, had shaken her head, hoping that her embarrassment would be regarded as shyness. They left soon after lunch, everyone coming to see them off with laughter and teasing. Withdrawing into her corner while Bren put on speed, Serena wondered with a pang whether anything quite so nice would ever happen to her again. She doubted it. The ring on her finger felt heavy and strange and speech was beyond her at the moment.

'Not bad, was it?' Bren began conversationally as he gave attention to the road ahead. 'Everything went off well, including the arrangements I've made for opening an account for you at the bank through Dill.'

Serena blinked, not sure whether she had heard aright, and with a youthful dignity that sat well on her slender shoulders she sat bolt upright in her seat and stared at him as though he was out of his mind.

'You must be joking!' she cried indignantly. 'Why, I wouldn't touch a penny of your money! What do you think I am?'

'My wife,' he answered coolly.

'Your wife in name only,' she scoffed, 'and that's all it amounts to. Why, you didn't even. . . .'

'Kiss you?' he cut in, tossing her a look on uplifted brows. 'Did you want me to?'

Serena went scarlet. So he had known about it.

She said scathingly, 'What do you think? I don't want your money either. Thanks all the same,' she sighed exaggeratedly. 'I suppose I'm lucky to be able to trust you. That's payment enough.'

He said irritably, 'Don't be so complacent about it. I'm only a man with a normal man's reactions to a wide-eyed, slender, silky-haired chick.'

'Thanks,' she snapped. 'That's the first time I've been called a wide-eyed, slender, silky-haired chick, and I can't say that I care for it. Sorry I'm not the more sophisticated type, a true blue Aussie, for instance, like Sadie.'

Forcibly, he said, 'You're evading the issue—and leave Sadie out of this. It's also irrelevant what kind of woman I prefer. Let's go back to the subject in hand, shall we? I've made a settlement on you and it stands.'

Serena lifted her chin, wishing she could control her heart as well as she could her voice.

'That's precisely what it will do—stand, because I shan't touch any of it. Furthermore, I'm perfectly capable of earning my own money my way.'

'What's the matter? Scared to take it in case I should ask for something in return? The important thing is you now have no problems.'

Serena bit her lip and gave her attention to the passing landscape. It held no magic for her any more and far from having no problems she would say that hers had increased with the weight of his ring on her finger. Eventually they would arrive at the Cockatoo where Bren would have ample time to make it up with Sadie. What happened between them would be their business. Serena Downs would only have a small part to play as his wife. All that talk about celebrating their wedding later on their return to Tamura was all part of the game of behaving normally. By that time she and Bren would have gone their separate ways, and nothing would be easier than for her to slip away out of his life and for him to seek an annulment.

The passing panorama of rolling scrub struck a note of desolation in her heart.

She said, 'Would it be premature to ask about any future plans you have in mind? I know we're staying at the Cockatoo until after the polo match. I suggest we both go our own way then. I—I mean, you go to your place and I continue on my travels.'

Carelessly, he answered, 'Most things have a way of panning out on their own without much of a push. Take it easy. You worry too much.'

Helplessly Serena gripped her hands on her lap. She felt

relegated to a minor employee of his who would be dispensed with at his will. His ego was king-sized if he thought she was willing to continue to be a pawn in his game of stalking his queen. Her life had become fraught with mixed emotions ever since his tall figure had loomed from the crowds of a Sydney street. Despite his assurances that their marriage was only one of convenience one could not deny that he had taken over the role of the piper who called the tune with a vengeance. Worse still, he was not going into any details as to how long their marriage was to go on.

Still engrossed in a situation she had agreed to so blindly, Serena was aware of the car engine behaving oddly. The next moment the car shuddered to a stop. Unfolding his long length from behind the wheel, Bren got out to see what the trouble was. Then he was bending down to talk to her through the open window of the car.

'I won't be long fixing the trouble. You can get out to stretch your legs, but don't wander far away,' he said on an air of command.

The air was hazy with heat when she left the car, armed with her camera. Around her were vast plains of scrub, the horizon seemed to be in another world and there was not a kangaroo in sight. A bad place to be lost in, she thought, but with Bren there it was an enchanted place. He was already taking the breakdown in his stride, fishing among a box of tools he had taken from the car boot.

Looking at the back view of his wide shoulders he was the personification of man's liberation. Women's Lib was something unheard of here. Since Serena's declaration to honour and obey him in the marriage service he seemingly had taken it literally. The little woman was to be told nothing of his plans and now he was ordering her to stay put. And this was only the beginning of their strange partnership.

But did she want it any other way? Serena was not sure about this. She looked round and strolled over to a giant anthill. It was twice as high as herself and she set her camera to take a picture. There was nothing much in the way of scenery to take pictures of, but she did manage to take one of Bren as he straightened from rummaging in the car toolbox. He wasn't to know, of course. It would never do for him to guess at the reason why she had taken it. The print when developed would be put away with all her other treasures to look back upon with bitter-sweet pain.

There were several stumps of bottle trees, twisted and gnarled, and Serena strolled to a flat-topped one to sit down and look around patiently for some sign of kangaroos. But there were none to be seen. She closed her eyes and wondered what Dee was up to, whether her mother was still very ill or whether it had been a ploy for her to get her daughter back home. Maybe, as Bren said, she would never return. Well, at least her own journey here had not been in vain. She planned to see a lot more of the country before returning home.

Suddenly an arm whipped round her and she was whisked off the stump as a snake, a mere thrust of its tongue away from her, withdrew and slid into a crevice of the stunted tree.

'Idiot!' Bren's voice rasped in her ear. 'Did you have to sit down and make yourself an easy target for one of our poisonous snakes? We do happen to carry snake venom and antidotes with us, but we don't go out looking for excuses to use them!'

He put her down on her feet and glancing up at his face Serena saw he had gone a little grey beneath his tan.

'I'm sorry,' she mumbled, 'I'm afraid I was dreaming.'

He placed his hands carelessly on narrow hips and surveyed her with the large hat pushed at the back of his thick hair.

'And you reckon you'd be all right hopping around this country alone?' he scoffed with a vigour that brought the hot colour to her face. 'You'd never make it.'

Serena, resenting his tone, lifted a determined chin. 'Like to bet?' she challenged. 'I'm not afraid of wild life of any kind. I know it's been put on the earth for a useful purpose.'

Some of the anger left his face, but his nostrils were still a little dilated. His sudden change of colour puzzled her, since she would never believe that he could be so concerned about her. Yet she could have sworn to greyness around his mouth and nose seconds ago as he had placed her on her own two feet. But he looked all right now and that arrogance, that lazy nonchalant way, was back again in full force.

'Come on,' he said curtly as his hands dropped and he reached out to take her elbow. 'I shan't rest easy until I have you back again in the car.'

Before he let her get in he put his head inside the interior to scan the floor and the seats for crawlers. Then he helped her in. Serena moved to her corner away from him and Bren eyed her with his tongue in his cheek after sliding in beside her.

'While I admire your love of wild life there are lots of creatures around that you can't play ring-o'-roses with and live to tell the tale. So bear that in mind, will you?'

She nodded. 'I'm sorry for being so careless, and I want to thank you for what you did just now.'

He said dryly, 'You don't have to thank me for saving myself a heap of trouble. A bite from that particular kind of snake would have meant taking you to the nearest hospital after I'd treated it. That would not only have taken us out of our way, we would have been hours late at the Cockatoo.'

And Sadie. Serena was tempted to add those two final words since she was convinced that he was dying to get back to the Cockatoo and his love. Her voice shook slightly and she addressed her hands in her lap.

'But it didn't happen, did it? How does it feel to be tied to an idiot who can't scent danger when it's right under her nose?'

'I'll survive,' he answered.

In the silence which followed Bren made no attempt to

start the car. Instead he stared down at her bent profile. He spoke tolerantly.

'I guess now is as good a time as any to give you my wedding present before we proceed to the Cockatoo. They'll naturally want to know what my gift to you is.'

He pulled out a packet from his pocket and gave it to her, and the corners of his mouth lifted at her look of astonishment and dismay.

'But I have nothing for you,' she gasped. 'I—I never thought that far ahead. I—I hope it's nothing expensive— but then it doesn't really matter, does it, since I shall return it when our contract ends?'

He gave a careless shrug. 'Keep it as a memento. Go on, open it.'

Serena swallowed on a dry throat and opened the small package. The broad bracelet in heavy beaten gold was beautiful, and she gasped again.

'It's lovely!' she said on regained breath.

She watched as though mesmerised while Bren bent sideways to clip it on to her wrist.

'Slender wrist, slender ankles,' he drawled cynically. 'You'd be more at home in a beauty salon instead of in the outback.'

'Thanks, I'll bear that in mind when I receive any proposals from poor lonely Aussies.' The eyes she lifted to his were deep blue pools free of guile. Her smile was impish. 'According to your Aunt Julia single girls are in great demand in the outback.'

Bren glared at her. He was not amused—far from it. 'Don't give me that stuff,' he snorted. 'You aren't a single girl, in any case. You're a married woman—and don't you forget it. And don't let me find you playing around with any man while you wear my ring.'

She said demurely, 'Where's that sense of humour now?'

His reply was to set the car off at an appalling speed. With anyone else behind the wheel Serena would have felt scared, but this was Bren who had been angry at the thought of her dating another man. She lowered her eyes to the bracelet on her wrist. A bracelet and a photograph of him to comfort her in the barren years ahead when Australia was but a memory. The souvenirs were mounting up, and she wasn't sure that she wanted them to.

The thought occurred that she ought to have kissed him for the gift. A peck on that tanned cheek would not have been out of place. But he was the kind who wanted no thanks. Like the kiss he had omitted to give her at the wedding, he would regard it as uncalled-for. Their partnership had to be kept on a platonic basis, which should prove easy for him since Serena Downs held no great attraction for him as a woman. Sadie was more in his line with her mocking sophistication and provocative ways. A full-blooded man like Bren would enjoy mastering her and Sadie would revel in it. Serena lay back in her seat and closed her eyes. She would put the bracelet away and return it to him when they parted.

Later they stopped again, this time for refreshment, sandwiches, fruit and a delicious drink of homemade crushed pineapple, one of the Harrises' specialities. Neither of them spoke much. Bren was intent upon getting back to the Cockatoo and Serena was beginning to wilt after a somewhat unusual and tiring day.

Before he started the car Bren withdrew the flower from his buttonhole and tossed it into the glove compartment of the car. Then he smiled down at her.

'Good thing there wasn't any confetti to give the game away,' he drawled. 'How does it feel to be a married woman?'

'Rather constricting,' she confessed. 'But it's a big country.'

He said nothing but fixed her with a steady regard as though he could read her inmost thoughts. Serena quivered, wishing he did not look so strong and invulnerable. He was the ideal companion for a tour of the country, in tune as he was with all of its moods. But she knew, sinkingly, that he would only keep her with him for as long as it suited him.

'That's right,' he said. 'Keep your sense of humour and everything will be fine.'

Her tiredness was stretching her nerves to breaking point and she felt like laughing hysterically. If only she could treat the situation as fun!

'I'm dying with laughing,' she replied sarcastically.

'You're tired.' He started the car. 'When we reach the Cockatoo you must go straight to bed. Try to sleep.'

Serena could not possibly have slept; she had gone past it. Tremulously, her gaze strayed to the glove compartment and Bren's discarded buttonhole. She had given her own wedding spray of flowers to Luella since she had been the only single woman present at the wedding. Luella had been overcome with emotion and excitement, especially when Bren had kissed her cheek on their departure. Surreptitiously she had wiped away a tear, and Serena had been glad that Bren had seen fit to kiss the woman in appreciation of her services. The kind action made him seem more human and she wondered, idiotically, whether he would keep the buttonhole as a souvenir.

It was dark when they arrived at the Cockatoo station. This time they were not greeted by a blaze of lighted windows. The only light was a golden torch-like beam coming from the open doorway where Julia stood outlined in the aperture having heard the car. There was the usual greeting from the dogs, but Serena was too dead beat to respond much to their exuberance.

'Welcome back,' said Julia cheerfully. 'Had a nice day?'

She came forward to kiss Serena on the cheek and walked in between them to the open door. Bren replied in monosyllables, commenting on the quietness.

'Everyone gone to bed?' he asked.

'Everybody has gone to the Millers' barbecue,' Julia said, slanting a glance at his unrevealing profile. 'Did you forget they were giving their usual barbecue this evening? They were very disappointed because you were away for the day. I told them you might go over later, when you got back.'

'Forget it,' Bren gave his aunt a smile which robbed his

words of any offence. 'Serena is tired.'

Julia looked down rather jadedly at Serena's paleness, at the dark smudges beneth her deep blue eyes, and the downward sweep of thick lashes against the sudden light in the hall.

'I'll say she's tired. She looks all in,' she commented dryly. 'Really, Bren, you should remember that your wife is a city girl. She isn't used to our ways, and the outback can be very hard on her kind.'

Serena looked at her with a confused frown. She was at a loss to discriminate at the moment between kindness and bitchiness. Were Julia's remarks meant to tell Bren that he had married the wrong kind of girl? It certainly seemed that way to her. Maybe she was just overtired. The nearest thing to heaven that she could think of at the moment was crawling in between the sheets and seeking oblivion, in her own room.

Julia was saying, 'About your room—I'm afraid we haven't been able to do anything regarding a change of rooms. As you know, Bren, our guests are here until after the polo game on Saturday, so I can't turn any of them out. However, I've done the next best thing. I've put another bed in Serena's room to add to hers for a double one. Your room is too masculine, too austere for a bride. Had you told me sooner about your marriage things would have been different. But I'm sure you'll be comfortable, and you can always take a turn on the verandah if you feel cramped.'

'Thanks.'

Bren had moved behind his aunt and Serena felt herself being swept up into his arms. Before she could react he was striding away with her to their room. Once inside he set her down on her feet and switched on the light, then he strode to draw the curtains together at the windows. His actions shut them into a cocoon of warmth and cosiness which, far from allaying her fears, added to them.

Pulling herself together with an effort, she said quellingly, 'You didn't have to come over as a doting bridegroom and carry me here. I'm quite capable of using my own two feet.'

'Come on,' he murmured with a mock pained expression. 'You wouldn't deny a bridegroom the right to carry his wife across the threshold.'

'You didn't carry me over the threshold. This happens to be the bedroom, and—and I wish you'd stop behaving as though we were really married,' said Serena heatedly.

'But we are married, and we have to behave as if it was genuine, remember?' Bren strolled towards her. 'What with getting married and travelling for most of the time, it's been quite a day. You'll feel better after a good night's sleep.'

Serena gripped her handbag with trembling fingers. His low pleasant voice was setting up all kinds of vibrations inside her. Her whole frame quivered. She was not as afraid of him as she was of her own weakness in resisting him. Keep a sense of humour, he had said. She just could not.

She said stiffly, 'I'm afraid I don't find the situation as funny as you seem to do. In fact I don't find it funny at all.'

He said soberly, 'I can see you don't. You poor child, you're really afraid of me, aren't you?'

Quiveringly she hated him for his keen observation. 'You might put my mind at rest by telling me what you plan to do,' she answered weakly.

His slow smile lifted the corners of his mouth, endearingly, as though to put her at her ease. Instead it had the opposite effect with his magnetic charm making her break out into a cold sweat until she felt like screaming at him to get out.

'I suggest that you take a refreshing shower while I set about fixing our little love nest.' He raised an exasperated brow at her doubt-ridden expression and pushed his hands into his pockets before going on, 'Just to assure you that my intentions are honourable, I will now begin.'

Turning dismissively, he strode to the two beds which had been pushed together and made as one and proceeded to whisk off the covers. For seconds he held the flimsy nightdress he had uncovered in his hand before Serena pounced on it.

The hot colour burned her cheeks as she clasped the garment to her as she would something infinitely precious. Then as Bren began to move the two beds a distance apart, she went slowly to the bathroom. A session under the shower cleared her brain a little and by the time her nightdress was on she felt more alert.

Panic started when she looked around for her wrap to find that she had not brought it in the bathroom with her. Her nightdress was flimsy and much too revealing. The wrap was a necessity. For palpitating moments she stood holding her breath at the door striving to hear sounds coming from the next room. Bren had been whistling, but now all was quiet.

Would he go out now to fetch a tray or something? After all, they had not eaten since the last snack in the car that afternoon and it was now well after eleven o'clock. Serena put her ear to the door in an effort to find out what he was doing, but there was no sound. After a while it occurred to her that she could not stand there all night. Her whole body drooped with fatigue.

'Are you there?' she called out at last desperately. 'If you are you might pass me my wrap. It's peach-coloured like my nightdress and rather flimsy.'

'Certainly.' She heard his deep stirring voice as he moved around the room. 'Where is it supposed to be?'

'Over the back of the chair by the bed,' she answered.

'Doesn't seem to be anywhere around,' he called after a pause. 'You'd better come and see for yourself.'

'But I can't. Find me something from the wardrobe, a woolly cardigan or something,' returned Serena emphatically.

'Why not? You have your nightdress, haven't you? I take it that little bit of frippery you snatched up was your nightdress?'

She fumed at the mentality of the average male and stiffened as a knock came on the door.

'Just a minute—someone at the door. Probably our supper.'

At his words, Serena moved swiftly, aiming to get across the bedroom to her wardrobe and find a wrap of some kind. Opening the bathroom door, she streaked across the bedroom saw him turning from the door with a tray and, backing, slipped into one of the beds.

'That was quick,' he remarked, closing the door and moving forward with the loaded tray to the small table he had placed in readiness between the two beds. 'Did you find your wrap? Ah, I see you didn't.'

He raised a provocative brow at Serena sitting up in bed and clutching the bedcover up over her chest. Above the lace straps of her nightdress her creamy shoulders and the youthful line of her neck had the sheen of magnolia petals. The blonde streaky hair was sprinkled with gold dust from wall lights and her eyes were deep blue eloquent pools fixed upon his face.

Slowly he bent down over her, placing his hands down on the bed to support him.

'I don't know why you're looking at me as if I was some frightening creature from outer space,' he growled. 'I'd stop putting ideas into my head if I were you. Hell, what's this?' He looked down on the floor at his feet and bending down whipped up a heap of frothy pink négligé which he dropped scornfully on the bed. 'Your missing wrap, I believe. For Pete's sake put it on and let's have things normal around here. I don't know what all the fuss is about. After all, we are married.'

Serena shrugged hastily into the wrap and sat up straight in the bed.

'Please don't be more objectionable than you have to be,' she said primly.

'Objectionable? Me? Furthermore, there isn't the slightest need for you to be afraid of me. For one thing, you aren't the type I'd choose as a passing fancy. For another, you're the delicately boned kind whose vulnerable appearance appeals instinctively to a man's better nature. So stop regarding me as the big bad wolf.' He drew himself up to stare down at her with hard eyes. 'And now I'll take a shower.' He gestured to the tray. 'Help yourself.'

When he had gone to the bathroom, Serena pushed herself up further in the bed and reached out to the tray to pour herself coffee from the percolator. It was good. It was hot but she did not lift the cloth covering the food. Even a mouthful would have choked her. She was so tired, and within minutes of having the drink she was snuggled down and fast asleep.

CHAPTER SEVEN

SERENA was awakened by the door opening and closing. The hour was late, she could tell by the heat from the sun penetrating the room. Hers had been the sleep of exhaustion, but she was awake enough now, awake enough to push herself up in the bed and focus on the tall, wide-shouldered figure approaching her side of the bed with a tray.

Bren was dressed in his moleskins, elastic-sided boots and big hat. Beneath the brim his face looked more chiselled than ever as he moved with that lazy synchronisation of active muscles. He crossed the room in a couple of strides and laid the tray down on her knees.

His greeting was skilfully casual. 'Had a good night?' he asked, and pushed the hat to the back of his head as he looked down at her.

Last night she had been aflame with the desire to call him hard names, until he had cut her down to size by telling her where she stood in his affections. She would have preferred to have been able to prepare herself for meeting him again.

'Yes, thanks. I never wakened all night,' she said, aware of her tousled hair. 'Did you?'

He looked down at her whimsically. 'I always sleep well. Now if you'll excuse me I'll take a shower. I've been doing a job of work.' He strode across the room and looked round at the bathroom door. 'I've brought an extra cup for coffee. I had breakfast earlier, but I'll enjoy a drink.'

Serena had eaten her breakfast and enjoyed it by the time he returned. He leaned back against the dressing table on her side of the bed and accepted his drink politely.

He said soberly, 'I owe you an apology for last night. I

106

had no right to speak to you as I did. After all, you're doing me a favour, a big one, and I shouldn't have blown my top.'

Serena's voice was clear and perfunctory. It gave the impression she intended, of total indifference.

'That's all right,' she said. 'Nice to know where you stand.'

Bren drank part of his coffee and smiled. 'Good thing our marriage isn't the real thing. Still, it makes good practice for when the genuine thing comes along.' He rubbed the side of his nose thoughtfully with a long brown finger and smiled at her tousled head and flushed cheeks. 'I can tell you one encouraging thing. You look very sweet first thing in the morning when you wake, and you're a perfect beauty when you're asleep,' he said wickedly.

Her eyes were an extraordinary deep blue in the soft rose of her face.

'I don't think that was fair,' she protested. 'It was a mean thing to do, to study me when I was asleep.'

'Don't worry,' he replied ironically. 'I had to concentrate on your face in case I wakened you by pushing the beds together again. We have to keep up appearances, and I hated the thought of waking you so early after you were so dead beat last night.'

He emptied his cup and Serena refilled it with the last of the coffee, feeling mean and petty.

'I'm sorry.' She made a thing about finishing the rest of her drink. 'Did you have to go out?'

'Not really, but I usually give a hand while I'm here.'

'Where did you go?'

An ironic smiled twitched his lips. 'Lesson number one. Never begin to assert your conjugal rights on your wedding morn by asking your husband where he's been. I wouldn't advise it.'

Serena consulted her watch and saw that it was well after eleven o'clock. 'Did you go out riding?' she asked. It was a great temptation to mention Sadie, but she resisted it.

'Yes, kind of,' laconically.

With the feeling that he was putting her off, she insisted. 'As we aren't really married and as I propose to learn about marriage when I sample the real thing I'm still curious as to where you went.'

Bren looked at her over the rim of his cup as he drained it.

'You'll be sorry you asked so soon after your breakfast,' he warned.

She said indignantly, 'You haven't been shooting kangaroos, have you?'

He shook his head. 'Still want to know?'

She nodded.

He put down his empty cup on the tray, then removed it from the bed on to the dressing table. Serena watched him in silence as he leaned back in his original position against the table and proceeded to roll a cigarette. Taking his time, he lit it, exhaled a line of smoke towards the ceiling, then looked at her with a narrowed gaze.

'I have no idea how much you know about the outback, but we happen to have a particular pest known as a blow-fly. Unfortunately it attacks sheep and although we drench them thoroughly to prevent this happening a certain number of sheep get flyblown. When this happens we have to round them up to shear off the flyblown wool to get rid of the maggots.' He grinned wickedly as she flinched. 'You'd enjoy the willy wagtails sitting patiently on the fence for a good feed.'

Serena had lost a little of her colour and was fighting off a feeling of nausea. 'Good feed?' she echoed weakly.

'Maggots.'

She covered her face with her hands in a shudder of revulsion.

'It's—horrible,' she mumbled into damp palms. 'I think I'm going to be sick.'

'Well, you would insist upon knowing where I'd been. I told you it was a mistake. Want me to carry you to the bathroom?'

Her head shot up out of her hands and she glared at him. 'Don't you dare!' she cried.

Unperturbed, he inhaled and exhaled from his cigarette with a nonchalance that increased her indignation. His eyes were intently and critically upon her, but they told her nothing.

He said evenly, 'I'm going to ride over to see some friends of mine. I'm not suggesting that you come with me because you won't feel up to it after yesterday. I'd like to think that you're taking it easy while I'm away.'

Serena swallowed uneasily, not relishing the idea of being left with Julia and Sadie. 'That's as good a way as any of telling me I'm not wanted.' she retorted.

The expression in his dark eyes changed to the kind one would give a child in a tantrum.

'Come if you want to. I can only warn you that it's a long ride for someone who's unaccustomed to it.'

She lowered her eyes from his magnetic gaze. 'I could take some photographs of animals and birds on the way. After all, it's the reason I came to this country—to see all I can of the life here.'

He said tolerantly, 'You'll be able to take all the photographs of the wild life you want at Tamura. There's more than enough there to quench your thirst for knowledge and adventure.'

It was on the tip of her tongue to tell him that she would not be going with him to Tamura. It was her intention to think of some excuse for ending their marriage before then. He would probably make a fuss about it, but at least no one would be hurt except herself, since she loved him so much. It would be like dying to leave him.

She was aware of him straightening from the dressing table to put his cigarette out in a nearby ashtray.

'See you later,' he said. 'Take it easy, and have a nice rest.'

Serena made no answer. The next moment she was alone. Later when Julia knocked on her door she was washed, dressed and putting the finishing touches to the room. The bed was neatly made, soiled towels and linen neatly folded ready to be collected and laundered.

Julia looked around the neat room approvingly. Her smile was friendly. Her eyes took in Serena's youthful glow and freshness.

'No need to ask if you had a good night,' she said. 'I came to ask if you wanted to do anything special today. Bren stressed the fact just now that you needed to rest.'

Serena's reply was tempered by the fact that it was necessary for her to play the part of the adoring and happy bride.

'I'd like to use my camera today taking pictures. What do you suggest?'

Julia said thoughtfully, 'Well now, some of the boys are riding out in the paddocks to repair fences, so you could go with them. They take a packed lunch, so you can stay out for the rest of the day, if that would suit you. Bren won't be back until supper time. Sadie is out too.'

Serena's heart lurched painfully as she pictured them riding together, Bren and Sadie. But wasn't that what she wanted? The sooner they made it up the sooner Serena Downs could live as a normal person again instead of being laid open to all the painful emotions of unrequited love.

'I'd like that very much, thanks,' she said, and managed a warm smile as though her heart was in it.

Julia introduced her to the stockmen, two of whom, Joe and Ben, were to go with her to the paddocks. Actually, Joe and Ben were called fencers. They worked continually maintaining the fencing and gates of the paddocks. Serena was mounted on one of the stock horses, and thoroughly enjoyed herself. She pumped the two men dry of information during their lunch break, listened attentively to their yarns and chased kangaroos, eventually succeeding in taking some really good pictures. The birds were beautiful in their coloured plumage, and she took endearing pictures of willy wagtails and thought poignantly of Bren.

They returned to the homestead and Serena went to her room to wash and change for supper. Joe and Ben, after seeing her back, returned to their own quarters somewhere out on the paddocks. Bren was not there, and she gave a sigh of relief to have the opportunity of taking a bath and changing in his absence. She was ready at last and another hour went by slowly. There was still an hour to go before supper and Serena felt annoyed with herself for having hurried in getting ready.

Pacing the room, she amused herself by trying to imagine what she might have been doing had she not met Bren. For one thing, she would not be at the Cockatoo. She would be staying in the outback at some small one-horse town like the one near to the polo fields they were going to on the following Saturday, or at someone's homestead. But she would have been free, free to please herself whether to go to a function or to stay in for the night, after a strenuous day, curled up in a comfortable chair with her favourite book. What was more, the film in her camera would now be in some enterprising developer's hands to be ready for her the following day.

The homestead was quiet but her nerves were jumpy. Serena stopped her pacing and, suddenly fearful of Bren striding in and her own vulnerable reaction to his appearance, she decided to go out on to the verandah in order to see him arrive. That way she could prepare herself for his coming. The cool clear air met her like a draught of thirst-quenching liquid.

The scent of frangipani came pleasantly to the nostrils with the golden sunset lingering on the far horizon like some exotic woman in a gown of changing colours reluctant to take her final bow to the inevitable night. Soon the sky would be a pale opal, cattle in the paddocks would loom silhouetted against it and the arid smell of earth would predominate.

'If you're looking for Bren you're wasting your time. He won't come back tonight.'

The cool mocking tones coming from quite near startled Serena from her contemplation of the scene before her, and she turned slowly to see Sadie, hands high as they clasped a verandah post, eyeing her with scorn as she swayed from side to side.

Taken by surprise and shaken by the dislike in the girl's eyes, Serena heard herself saying breathlessly, 'Hello. I thought you were out.'

'You mean you hoped I wouldn't come back while you were here with Bren?'

'As a matter of fact I thought you were with Bren.'

Serena's frankness, the sweet steady gaze of her dark blue eyes, free of rancour, put Sadie out, but only for a moment. She laughed, a harsh laugh that hardened her features.

'Did you now? So I might have been if you hadn't set your cap at him. Easy prey, wasn't he, because I wasn't there? Well, I'll tell you something—you might have his ring, but you won't keep him.'

Serena could have agreed wholeheartedly. Instead she found herself seeing Sadie through Bren's eyes. No one could deny her beauty, the graceful curve of arms reaching out for the post, the lovely profile thrown into relief as she threw back her head and continued to sway provocatively from side to side. A necklace and matching ear-rings of crystal stabbed the fading light and the wisps of chiffon floated back from her slender figure outlining the curves. The overall impression was that of a naughty, spoiled child of the kind that made one's fingers itch to chastise. Bren was right: Sadie needed teaching a lesson.

'Think so?' Serena's refusal to be angry again put Sadie off her stride, and as that young lady turned her head to give her an insolent appraisal with flashing eyes, Serena smiled.

'Poor Bren! No one could mistake you to be anything but English.' Sadie's voice, dipped in venom, added further offence. 'There's no bigger castastrophe for a grazier than for him to choose the wrong kind of wife.'

'Really?' Serena said mildly. 'Bren was most anxious for us to marry.' By way of a retort which she found impossible to resist, she added, 'He also reassured me that his wife would not be expected to be a stockman on the station. He certainly found me suitable, otherwise he wouldn't have married me.'

'But of course you knew all that when you married one of the wealthiest men in the outback,' Sadie retorted.

Serena's hold on the verandah rail tightened. She had to summon all her control to say, 'Bren isn't wealthy.'

'So he didn't tell you?' Sadie's voice held a triumphant note. 'Seems he's fooled you all along the line, even to allowing you to cherish fanciful illusions about his love for you. You know, I could be kind to you and tell you not to raise false hopes or romantic notions where Bren is concerned.'

'You're speaking about my husband,' Serena reminded her evenly.

Sadie's little smile came and went. 'And also the man I always understood that I would marry. Perhaps I ought to be more explicit. Will you understand me when I say that Bren's feeling for me is vastly different from his feeling for you?'

Serena spoke with dry irony. 'I appreciate the fact that having grown up together you and Bren would be close. It has occurred to me, though, that you could have overrated Bren's feelings for you, which are perhaps those of a brother more than a lover. Do you really and truly love him, Sadie?'

Sadie stopped swinging by her hands from the verandah post and eyed her insolently.

'What do you think? However much I love Bren it's nothing to how he loves me. Why, he's even gone to extraordinary lengths like marrying you to prove it. Why do you think he married you?' she taunted. 'Because he wanted to shake me. I've kept putting him off—I wanted to have a good time before I settled down.' She gave a brittle hard laugh that matched the hardness in her eyes. 'The joke is I was going to tell him I'd marry him here at the Cockatoo when he came from Sydney after the Show.'

'And in the meantime he married me. Hard luck!'

Whatever Serena had felt in the way of sympathy for Sadie had been swept away by the girl's revealing her true character. Her kind were well equipped to look after themselves. They grabbed their happiness from other people regardless of the hurt they brought in the process. There was no beating about the bush with Sadie and she, Serena Downs, was right in the middle of an absurd love tangle if what she said was true. Well, the sooner it ended the better for all concerned. Like Sadie, Bren was well able to take care of himself. Sadie was speaking again.

'I'd say it was hard luck for you being saddled with a husband who doesn't love you. I'd even go as far as to say that he's never really made love to you—which, I might add, he does beautifully.' She laughed again at the mounting colour in Serena's face. 'Don't look so shocked. I can see he hasn't. Now that's very encouraging.'

Serena stared at her gravely. She was horrified, repelled and yet managed to keep cool since it was obvious that Sadie was baiting her into talking about her marriage. She was playing a desperate game in order to get back the man she loved—or was it wanted? With Sadie it could be both. Her kind usually wanted whatever they couldn't get.

She said slowly, 'You don't know anything about our marriage. You're only surmising. Go ahead—try to break up our marriage, only before you do I'm sure Bren would want to see you less of a spoiled brat and more like the wife a grazier should have. Maybe if you'd been more like his ideal in the past all this wouldn't have come about— I don't know. All I know is that Bren and I are married and it will be up to us, not you, what we make of it.'

Sadie's lips thinned. Her eyes blazed. 'You little fool! You really think that Bren prefers you to me? Well, we'll see. Like I said, he won't come back tonight—that should prove whether he loves you or not. After all, you are supposed to be on your honeymoon. Go to sleep tonight with that thought for a nightcap!'

With this Sadie turned on her heel and went indoors. Her footsteps had hardly died away when Julia came out, looked along the verandah and seeing Serena, came forward.

'There you are, my dear. Bren has just been in touch. He won't be coming back tonight.'

Serena knew a faint relief, yet she would have given anything for Bren's reassuring presence after the venom of Sadie's attack. The girl was going to smile smugly when she heard, since Bren's absence was only proving the truth of what she had said against him. On the other hand, Bren would be tickled pink to know that his plan to punish Sadie was having an effect. She was aware of Julia taking her arm.

'We're having a barn dance after supper. I don't suppose you've done any barn dancing since you arrived, but don't worry, you'll soon pick it up. You'll find plenty of young men eager to teach you.'

There were. The floor of a large barn behind the homestead had been cleared, and the wooden floor waxed. The wild activity was something Serena needed desperately to keep her mind occupied. She put all thoughts of Bren behind her and looked upon the evening as only being one of many in the future when Bren and she had parted. In the square dancing Joe and Ben, her two companions of that afternoon, took it in turn to teach her all the whirls and sidestepping.

Naturally light on her feet and with a love for dancing, Serena soon moved around in tune with the rest. An amateur pop group provided the music and everyone joined in with gusto. The rafters rang with the stamping of feet and the clapping of hands, and presently Serena fell into the arms of the Cockatoo manager, Walt Field.

'You tread a pretty measure, ma'am,' he said, smiling down into her flushed face as the dance ended. 'May I have the pleasure of the next dance?'

Serena looked up into his pleasant face and wondered whether he wore the smart moustache for vanity or for business, since it gave him an air of well-groomed authority.

'If you wish,' she answered with a smile. 'If it's to be another square dance like the last I'm not very well up on it yet.'

'I'm sure it's going to be a waltz,' he told her. 'I hope so, since it will give me an excuse to take you in my arms. I saw you today out with Joe and Ben using your camera to good effect. By the way, I dabble in photography myself. Would you like your film developed?' He grinned, showing white teeth beneath the small clipped moustache. 'I'm not pushing for business. In this hot weather films are best developed as soon as possible.'

The music had begun again and it was a waltz. Serena glided round in his arms and glowed up at him.

'Would you really develop my film for me?' she asked as if it was too good to be true. 'I'd be so happy if you would. As a matter of fact, I was wondering who to ask, and Bren is away.'

She congratulated herself on the ease with which Bren's name slipped out as though they really were married.

'I'd be very happy to be of some service, Mrs Robart,' replied Walt.

The sound of her married name on his lips moved her oddly. Joe and Ben had addressed her thus several times that afternoon, but the sound of it still moved her. Since the dance had begun Serena had really begun to enjoy herself. Walt was a good dancer and he stayed with her for several more dances. It was only when memories of Bren were alerted by someone addressing her as his wife that a shadow seemed to hover over her evening's enjoyment.

So far Sadie had not been dancing and it was quite late when she came into the barn and looked around sulkily at the dancers. Serena had just finished her last dance with Walt, who had gone to an improvised bar to fetch some refreshment. With a tightening up of her reflexes, she looked Sadie right in the eye to assume a careless attitude she was far from feeling. If she was to enjoy her stay at the Cockatoo Sadie would not have to mean anything to her—Bren either, for that matter.

It was very late, around four in the morning, when the dance finished. Walt Field came to her at the door of the barn.

'I'll walk you across to the homestead, Mrs Robart, and you can give me the film you want developed. I shall be out in an hour or so mustering the cattle. Did you enjoy it?'

'Very much.' Serena lifted her face and breathed in the cold night air. 'I rather think we enjoy the unexpected more than the expected. I didn't know about the dance until just before supper.'

He said, 'I agree. Bren probably found you so unexpected that he was floored on sight. He's a lucky-so-and-so—but then he's a grand guy and a perfect beaut of a boss.'

The mention of Bren sent a quiver through her. It seemed that she was not to get away from him even in his absence.

Tremulously, she asked, 'His place, Tamura—what's it like? Is it very big?'

They were mounting the verandah steps and her face was averted.

'You said just now that the unexpected is more enjoy-able than the expected, so I won't spoil your pleasure by telling you anything about it. Bren can do that much better than I can. I will tell you this, though, his cattle and wheat are the finest in the outback.'

Walt had spoken slowly and sincerely, and Serena ad-mired him for it. What he was not to know was that she did not intend to see Tamura, having made up her mind to part from Bren at the first opportunity.

'If you come along the verandah I can go into the room by the french window to fetch the film,' she said, and sped along in front of him.

In seconds she was out again with the film in her hand. Walt took it and she said warmly,

'It really is good of you to do it for me. I'm simply dying to see the pictures I took of the kangaroos and the birds. By the way, there are several of Joe and Ben, the fencers. Could you do two of them so I can give them one?'

'Will do,' he answered. He turned as though to go, then

paused. 'May I wish you and Bren every happiness, Mrs Robart? I think it's a foregone conclusion that two such splendid people can't help but be happy. I'll let you have the film back this evening.'

CHAPTER EIGHT

NOBODY did anything strenuous on the day following the barn dance. Many of the guests did not get up for breakfast and had a belated lunch. In the afternoon some of them strolled lethargically to the tennis courts while others went out riding or played cards on the cool verandah.

Serena washed her hair and went for a ride after lunch as far as the tiny village where she posted letters and bought one or two mementos from the small general store which sold everything from food to household and farm equipment. She took a photograph of the small hotel, a real bushman's place. There was nothing remarkable about it except that it was the only one for miles, a square dull-looking wooden building that looked as though the men who had built it did it quickly in order to go inside for a drink.

She was in a world of her own taking the picture, and almost dazzled by strong light. At the moment she was utterly relaxed doing the thing she had wanted to do since coming to this strange and wonderful country.

An old-timer with pewter-coloured hair and a lantern jaw sat on the verandah of the hotel. He was a loose-limbed walnut of a man with bushy eyebrows and craggy features, but his eyes still gleamed with a kind of un-quenchable fire. Just the kind of Australian to give her picture some character.

Serena smiled at him, hoping he did not mind her taking his picture, and was rewarded with a beam of such genuine goodwill that she concluded that some gesture was called for. From him she learned that the hotel took a beating each night with at least three fights among the customers. If every now and then some drunk, in a mad moment, did not draw a gun and take pot shots at all the glass in sight including

119

the bottles on the shelves, people began to worry that things were getting dull.

Serena laughed at the old-timer's tales, took a peep into the hotel to see mellowed wood and a quiet atmosphere pervading in a well used room. Whether his stories were true or not, she did not linger to find out, and she rode leisurely back to the Cockatoo.

Sadie was conspicuously absent at supper and Serena had not seen her all day. Bren had not returned either and Serena decided to have an early night. In her room she changed into her négligé and curled up in a comfortable chair to read a little before going to bed.

It was after eleven when someone tapped on the verandah door. Serena had been trying to lose herself in the paperback chosen at random from those on her bedside table, and was about to give it up and go to bed. Wondering who it could be and knowing that Bren would have come in had it been he, she slipped on a wrap and opened the door.

'Hope I haven't disturbed you,' said Walt Field. 'I saw your light and thought you'd like the photographs. They're very good—not one bad one in the whole film.'

'Come in,' said Serena. 'I must pay you for developing them.'

Walt stepped inside and smiled awkwardly. 'I know it's kind of late, but I had to see Julia on business this evening so I brought the pictures with me. No, no!' He put up a protesting hand as Serena opened her purse. 'I want no payment. The pleasure is mine.'

He gave her the envelope and Serena made small protesting noises. But he was adamant.

'Bren not back yet?' he asked, noticing that she was alone.

She shook her head. 'Thank you,' she said. 'It was most kind of you to come and bring them so quickly and without charge.'

He left the room as quietly as he had entered, leaving Serena to close the door behind him. The pictures were good. There were two of herself, one taken with Joe which

Ben had taken and one taken with Ben which Joe had taken. Their horses were grazing by and one of the dogs from the Cockatoo was sitting beside her.

She had replaced them in the envelope and put them in her handbag when the french window burst open and Bren strode in. For long moments she stared at him, incapable of coherent speech. She felt recklessly, childishly happy because he had come back. But there was no happiness on his face, and the moments ticked away as he stood leaning back against the closed french window raking her with his eyes.

'So you're back,' she said, not thinking, and not caring that she should.

His lips hardly moved. 'How long was he here?' he demanded, his eyes moving over her négligé-clad figure and the wrap she had flung on a chair just before his arrival.

She stared at him stupidly, sensing his anger. In spirit he had receded away from her with the speed of a jet. He was ice-cold, rock-hard, as he repeated the question.

The hairs at the back of her neck prickled as he leaned back with an insolent arrogance against the closed door. She blinked and faced him wide-eyed.

'Who?' she asked.

'Don't look so mystified. You know who. Was that get-up for his benefit?' He gestured with his head at the négligé and Serena drew herself up with outraged dignity.

'Have you been drinking?' she demanded shakily.

His insolent regard stung and bewilderment battled with anger as she sought for calmness and civility. Her heart lurched to see that he looked tired and fed up as he took off his hat, flung it on to the bed and shoved his hands into his pockets.

His voice rasped as he said slowly, dangerously, 'I might ask the same of you. At least it would explain why you're behaving in this irresponsible manner.'

'Charming!' Serena clenched her hands and looked him squarely in the face. 'What kind of a heel are you, to accuse a man like Walt Field of making love to your wife?'

'I'm not accusing him, I'm accusing you. No man, however honourable, is one hundred per cent woman-proof, especially if the woman is like you.'

'But you are, aren't you?' she shot at him in white-hot indignation. 'As a woman I don't move you at all. Why then should I move Walt?'

One moment they were glaring at each other, the next Bren was there, so close to her that she could smell his sweat sweetened by the tang of fresh clean air, the crushed grass on his elastic-sided boots, and the masculine aroma of good masculine grooming.

Quivering inwardly, Serena was wondering if she had ever possessed any will-power at all. Certainly there was none to summon right now when she was needing it so desperately. She was like one hypnotised at his nearness. Every bit of her was crying out as in a wilderness for him to take her in his arms and kiss her until she was breathless.

His arms reached out to grasp the delicate glowing shape of her arms in the peach négligé, and she held her breath as it seemed that he was responding to the desperate need in her and dew oozed on her temples.

Then the adrenalin of her will-power began to work. Where was her pride? Much as she wanted his kisses, Serena did not want those prompted by indignation and a sense of injustice. What had hurt him most was not that Walt had made love to her but that everyone regarded her as his wife. As such she must not besmirch the name of Robart. Black depression swept over her—but this was no time for procrastination.

She hardly recognised her own voice. 'Walt came to bring me some photographs he'd developed from a film I used yesterday. He wasn't here more than five minutes— ask your aunt Julia if you don't believe me. He brought them with him because he was calling on her this evening to talk business. No doubt he would mention to her that he was calling on me.'

Bren's hands dropped. Striding to the bed, he picked up his broad-brimmed hat, slung it on to his head and strode out of the room via the french window.

Still standing where he had left her, Serena felt the confusion inside her gathering in momentum, until her knees were shaking and she sat down on the bed to gather herself together. Another second and she would have been in his arms; it had been evident without any vestige of doubt.

With her face covered by her hands, she could not bear to think how she had clung to those rare precious moments that had fired her blood as he had reached out to her. Fool, she told herself, to have ever thought that she could ever have his kisses except in his anger. For all she knew of him, he could have a dozen women in his life.

For the second night in succession, Serena hardly slept. At half past five she could no longer stay in bed tossing and turning. Bren had not come back and she sat up in bed to reach for the photographs Walt had developed, resolving to give Joe and Ben theirs later. The photographs of the kangaroos were sweet, and there was a delicious one of a baby wallaby. She was smiling at it tenderly when the verandah sounded with the footsteps of the stockmen going into breakfast. She padded to the french window to look for Joe and Ben but they had all gone indoors.

Acting on a sudden impulse, Serena washed and dressed, tied a triangle scarf pirate-wise over her streaky blonde hair and went to the kitchen. Julia was helping Madris serve the generous helpings of food for the men, and Serena smiled to see Joe and Ben at the end of the long table near to the door.

As she stood diffidently in the kitchen doorway Julia turned from one of the cookers.

'Hello, Serena,' she cried on a note of surprise as she carried two loaded hot plates between oven gloves to the table. 'You are up early. Missed Bren, did you? He's back. Came back last night, but he didn't want to disturb you, so he slept with the boys.'

What with the noise of dishes, full and emptied, being swapped about, and the men's stentorian talk and laughter, Julia's voice was muted and most of the present company did not hear it. Serena was thankful for this and she hurriedly moved behind Joe and Ben as they sat together and laid the photographs beside their plates.

With heightened colour, she said, 'I wanted Joe and Ben to have their pictures.'

'But don't you want to see your husband?' Julia interposed. 'He's about to go out mustering with the stockmen.'

Guiltily Serena glanced down the long table, aware now that most of the men had stopped talking and that Bren was there eating his breakfast with the rest. Gone was the opportunity for her to cut and run before any of the men or Bren saw her. Julia's strident tones had rent the air like church bells on a silent morning. She could cut and run, but why should she, smarting as she was from Bren's treacherous barbs of doubt as to her decency?

After all, was not she Serena Downs who had come to Australia to tour the country? That being the case she would have taken mustering in her stride as one of her adventures. Her smile at Julia was disarming.

'Good—I'll go with them. I am ready.'

'You are not going.'

Bren's deep tones from way down the table smote her ears like a gong. Her legs were trembling so much she was glad to sit down at the end of the table between Joe and Ben. All eyes were on her now, an elf of a girl, slim and shapely with streaky blonde hair. The loose woollen sweater over the tailored silk blouse and the smart moleskin trousers left no doubt of that. Julia passed her her breakfast and she began to eat.

Julia went on with her task wisely saying nothing. She saw Serena's face looking a little pale, and the thick silky lashes against her cheeks as she concentrated on her plate. She saw Bren, lean and tanned, as enigmatic as ever, leaning back in his chair and rolling a cigarette.

By the time he had stubbed out his cigarette, Serena had left the table and had gone to her room for her camera.

As she came out she met Julia, who offered her a small stetson hat.

'Sadie's,' she said laconically. 'She won't need it today. I'll be surprised if she's up before noon. She came home with Bren last night after going to meet him.'

Serena's heart went cold. 'With Bren?' she echoed.

'Yep, you know Sadie. Does just what she likes. Anyway, it was some ride and she was tired when she came in.' Her look at Serena's downbent head as she accepted the hat was whimsical. 'Think you can make it?'

Serena quelled an inward quiver. 'If I don't Bren will be there to pick up the pieces.'

Julia shook her head. 'He's not going to like it.'

Suddenly Serena's head shot up. She said defiantly, 'That's just too bad, because I have a feeling that I shall.'

Later mounted on one of the stock horses waiting for the men she was not so sure. Where was her resolution now to see the country? It was not too late to back down. Yet why should she? What had got into her? What was more, how dared Bren sit in judgment of her as he had done last night? How dared he after being with Sadie and walking out of their room on his return to rejoin the girl again? How *dared* he?

Her heart was a hammer disobeying frantic messages for calm when the men came on their horses. There was Bren, tall in his saddle, looking steely-eyed and as cold as a glacier, and the rest of the men grinning from ear to ear. Serena moved her horse forward, refusing to look at Bren, and rode along with the men. Their job was to move sheep from one paddock to another some considerable distance away. The job could not be hurried as many of the sheep had newly born lambs, so the pace was slow and relaxed. The weather was glorious, hot but not burning since the heat was tempered by a slight breeze through the scrub.

They all stopped for a picnic lunch and Serena found herself sitting with Bren. She had enjoyed the morning's work holding her own with the others. Her horse was amiable and negotiable. Furthermore, she had not put a foot wrong.

The men were rolling their cigarettes when Bren said to no one in particular,

'Anyone who wants to drop out can do so. We shall be finished in an hour or so.'

Serena was not so naïve as not to know that he was getting at her. Futile to wish that Walt Field was there since he had gone off for the day on business for Julia. After a heart-jerking moment, she forced herself to gather her wits. Her cheeks were burning, a treacherous flush of colour that mortified and robbed her of speech. Her hands were trembling and it was certain that her voice would be too. By a great effort of will she steadied herself. She contemplated with dismay some anti-climax in which she would be in the middle.

'A good idea,' she said at last with a steady smile. 'You drop out, Bren, if you want to. We won't mind, will we, fellows?'

Her disarming smile at them all as they sat and lolled around on the ground was received with delighted grins.

'No, sirree!' they cried, and looked expectantly at Bren to see how he was going to take it.

Bren, however, remained more nonchalant than the men, but to Serena his manner radiated a sense of excitement in her growing apprehension. He was taking it far too calmly. But she did not care. He had asked for it. Competently he finished rolling his cigarette, lit it and leaned back on one elbow to enjoy the fragrance. Serena glanced his way wondering at his deadly composure and at the secret smile lifting the corners of his well-cut mouth. Maybe he was still nursing a hope that she might come a cropper in some way before they returned to the Cockatoo. Well, just let him. She would show him!

Around four o'clock they coaxed in the last of the sheep in their paddock and Serena took the opportunity to break away from the men and ride away. Fortunately they were all too engrossed in some of the baby lambs to notice her go. Her idea was to ride to the polo grounds and take a shower in the pavilion there, then to ride back casually to the homestead. There was an elderly stockman clearing up for the weekend match and he fetched out towels from a locked cupboard when she told him of her intention to take a shower.

He had gone when she emerged from the coolness of water drenched limbs. She had put on her moleskins and her bra and was sliding her shoulders into the silk tailored blouse when she heard firm strong footsteps. Her hands were shaking as she wrestled with the buttons on her blouse when a figure loomed in front of her, shutting out the sun.

Bren's eyes were on her, on her skin pink and glowing as a wild rose, and Serena felt the slow thudding of her heart threatening to choke her. Wide-eyed, she stared as with torturing deliberation he moved nearer.

He was smiling in a way that quickened her senses to a feeling of danger. Retreating a step, she cried, 'Hello. Have you come for a shower too?'

He said slowly, filling up her retreating step, 'I doubt if even a shower would cool me down enough. You've been asking for this all day.'

His hands were on her shoulders, pushing their way under the unfastened blouse to close over her soft flesh. His head bent to shut out the light and the thing she had yearned for so hopelessly happened. His arms closed around her beneath the blouse.

There was no love in the warm masculine arrogance of his mouth as it crushed her lips in a cruel kiss. His hands moved slowly over her back and Serena swooned in a pool of bliss. He kissed her again and again with a cruel deliberation which could have said, take this and this for having disobeyed my wishes, and for setting yourself against me in front of the men. His lips were like a powerful drug drowning all resistance, and Serena could only cling as his mouth moved into the softness of her neck.

Teetering on such emotional heights, she loved him so much she could have told him so. But this isn't love, a small voice insisted inside her. The voice was a cold call to reason. When his lips moved to her soft trembling mouth again there were tears in her eyes, and fearful lest he should see them, she tore herself away, blinking them back.

'You can't bear anyone to stand up to you, can you?' she accused him violently in a choked voice. 'You had to teach me a lesson to satisfy your own ego, plus the fact that I came with you and stood the test. Well, let me tell you, you great brute of an Australian, that any girl can be the wife of a grazier if she gives her mind to it—only she would have to be out of her mind to even consider it!' A small devil of anger prodded her on at the quirk of amusement on his lips. 'I must have been out of mine to consent to this farce with you!' Her fingers sought the buttons on her blouse and she thrust them into the holes, while her blue eyes, bright with unshed tears, glared at him. 'Or did you settle it all last night with Sadie when you stalked out of our room after insulting me?'

A mask of cold anger replaced the amusement on his face. His eyes flicked over her in calculated surprise.

'What do you mean?'

For one wild moment Serena hoped that Julia had been wrong about her daughter being with him last evening. But there was no softening in him.

'You heard,' she answered. When a small laugh floated in the air, she was surprised that it was hers. 'I'm certainly learning about the people and the country here.'

'Maybe I'm learning myself too. I've certainly learned something in the last five minutes. If I've been wanting to prove something, I've done that too,' he said grimly.

'Congratulations.' Flung from such emotional heights, she was in no state to question what he meant. Not that she could not guess. His kisses had told her that he had no love for her. Fool that she was to ever have thought that he might! She felt bruised and battered by the cruel grip of his arms and his merciless kisses, but most of all she felt humiliated in the way a girl does when a man shows that he does not want her. Suddenly it was too much to take.

Tears flooded her eyes, blurred her sight, and she hurried past him to where her horse stood waiting.

Within seconds she was up in the saddle and riding away like the wind as if a thousand devils were after her. Her horse seemed to be eager to return home too and thundered along with her neck outstretched and her powerful muscles rippling into their stride. It was not until the wind whistled through her hair that Serena realised she had left Sadie's hat behind at the polo pavilion. She was beginning to realise something else—that her horse was no longer under her control. Too late she tried to prevent the headlong pace, had seconds to see the closed gate ahead before they hit it. Serena cleared the gate, sailing over the horse's head to land with a sickening thud on her back that knocked the breath out of her body. Sky and earth were hinged as she fought against unconsciousness. The poor horse was her first coherent thought. Was she dead? Please God, no! Valiantly she struggled to her feet to see it gazing down at her with soft brown eyes. Tears of thankfulness rolled down her cheeks unheeded as she tottered forward, then somehow Bren was in her path between her and the horse.

Tremulously, she cried, 'She's all right! She isn't hurt. Aren't I glad?'

This time she did not feel the strength of his arms as he scooped her up and bore her away. She had fainted.

CHAPTER NINE

SERENA was in hospital for two days for X-rays and injections, during which time the slight concussion had cleared up. It was the result of the X-rays which shocked her. There was extensive bruising of her back and a very slight fracture of one vertebra. Riding, rough travel and all kind of strenuous activities were out for a time.

She had just heard the result of the X-rays when Bren strode in to lift an eyebrow at the tears in her eyes.

'Tears?' he scoffed. 'Come now, it isn't that bad, is it?'

Immediately on the defensive, she cried, 'That bad? You must be joking! Can't you see that I shan't be able to do any more travelling around the country until my back is better? I'll just have to go back to Sydney and take a job in an office again.'

'Why?' he answered coolly, lowering his long length into a chair beside her bed.

'Well, it's obvious, isn't it? I might even go back home if Dee doesn't show up.'

'Do you want to go home?'

'There isn't much point in staying, is there? Besides, isn't this the opportunity you've been waiting for? You've done what you wanted and taught Sadie a lesson by putting yourself out of her reach by our marriage. Believe me, that girl is going to appreciate you more from now on. She loves you.'

Bren looked startled. 'Does she now? Has she said so?'

'Not in so many words, but a woman can sense things in another woman that men can't.'

Bren had taken off his hat to perch it on his outstretched knees and he was staring down at it with a furrowed brow. A blockage in Serena's throat irritated and brought the

130

prickle of tears to her eyes. It was a great temptation to stretch out her hand and touch the dark, crisp hair. For the moment he looked young and vulnerable. If he had looked up then he would have seen the yearning in her eyes, but he was intent upon his own thoughts.

Bitterly it occurred to Serena that he must be feeling over the moon to know that Sadie loved him. By telling him she had brushed away all chance of making any headway with him herself. Maybe she could have made him love her. Even that kind of love brought on by feminine wiles would have been better than that she should lose him altogether. But with a sense of despair Serena knew that she was capable of deep, lasting love herself, and seeking love on the rebound would not satisfy her in the end. It would be dust and ashes in her mouth.

At last he said evenly, 'That's interesting, but shall we come back to the subject in hand? You.' He paused as though reaching a decision. 'I'm taking you with me to Tamura.'

She drew a quivering breath and gave her attention to the coverlet on her bed. Keeping her voice as steady as she could, she said on a low key,

'You might as well know I have no intention of going with you to Tamura. What's more, I don't think it's fair of you to expect me to. I—I'm of the opinion that this farce we're playing has gone far enough. Don't you think so?'

'Are you asking me or telling me?' he drawled.

She gave a wisp of a smile. 'A bit of both, I suppose, and —and you aren't helping me much, are you?'

He said curtly, 'It takes two to enter into a partnership, and two to break it.'

'You have my permission to end it,' she murmured. 'I— I'm only too happy to give it.'

As her fingers gripped the edge of the coverlet to prevent them quivering his ring shone mockingly up at her. She would miss it. Strange how she had become accustomed to wearing it. Soon her finger would be as empty without it as her heart.

Bren was speaking again in a deep voice loaded with sarcasm.

'And your being happy about it should make me happy too. Is that how you think? If you do then I must hasten to put you right. I don't feel happy about breaking our partnership at this stage.'

'But why?'

'I made a promise to show you the country under my protection, and I'm sticking to that promise. You're going to Tamura to further your knowledge of life in the outback. Social life here is not as dull as you might imagine. We have as much fun in our way as the slick city guys. At Tamura, there's swimming in the river, tennis, riding, polo, visits to an elegant hotel not far away, with occasional trips into the big cities for shopping sprees and business.'

Serena closed her eyes. With Bren in command it sounded like heaven, but it was not for her. Once she was there it would be much harder to break away and cut adrift from him. She had not that kind of courage since her love for him was growing more each day, and because she was so emotionally involved she interposed roughly.

'That's very kind of you and I appreciate it, but I'm not a hundred per cent fit, so I must refuse. I'm quite determined to go back to the city.'

Slowly he turned his head to give her a pained smile. 'And that, I take it, is your last word?'

Serena nodded, unable to trust her voice. He shrugged wide shoulders, giving the impression that he had done his best.

'If that's what you want,' he said, somehow making it final. Rising to his feet with that loose unconscious grace of movement so typical of him, he strode to the door to summon the nurse.

Next time he came to the ward Serena was dressed and ready. With a lurch of her heart she could imagine the attention he received on his arrival at the hospital, this very tall, very handsome man with long legs, a bronze tanned face, easy movements, and a slow drawl. Gracefully she walked beside him into the bright sunlight. There was an ambulance waiting and Bren climbed into it with her.

Was the acute wave of disappointment washing over her because he had taken her decision without putting forward further argument? Serena was too confused to admit it. All she could think about was that Bren would be returning to Tamura on his own and going out of her life for ever. The thought was almost too much for her to bear. Feverishly she wondered whose idea it was for her to have an ambulance. Probably the doctor, who had stressed the need for her to take it easy by not travelling rough. There was no doubt about her back recovering, but her heart never would. In an effort to appear normal, she said by way of conversation,

'Did you play polo?'

'Yes,' laconically.

'Did your side win?'

'Yes.'

'I'm glad. I'd like to think that I've brought you luck. After all, it's these little things like winning at polo which make your day.'

'Oh, sure.'

In the uneasy silence that followed Serena felt him retreating miles away from her in spirit, and the atmosphere became so intense that she felt like screaming.

She said compulsively, 'I'm sorry I can't say goodbye to your aunt Julia and everyone at the Cockatoo. Perhaps you'll thank them for me. There's my suitcase too. I'll arrange to have it sent on when I find somewhere to stay in Sydney.'

'I've already done everything,' he assured her. 'I had the result of your X-rays long before you did, and I came to the hospital today fully prepared. I know you only too well, and this independent attitude of yours is completely in character. Nobody is going to offer you warm hospitality while you recuperate, over your dead body. It hasn't occurred to you, has it, that you might be robbing people of the pleasure of putting you up while you recover from the fall?'

'You're making me out to be a perfect little beast,' she cried, blushing furiously. 'Look, I'm not ungrateful. I've had a gorgeous time at the Cockatoo and everyone has been wonderful to me—but you can't go staying with someone for weeks on end. It isn't fair. Everyone works so hard out here and I refuse to add to their chores.'

'All right. You've made your point—forget it.'

As he spoke the ambulance turned sharply to the left, cruised along for some distance, then turned in an arc before coming to a halt. Bren opened the door, jumped out and lifted her down.

They were on an air-strip and right in front of her was the cutest small plane she had ever seen. The ambulance driver returned Bren's salute and drove away, and Serena lifted bewildered wide blue eyes to Bren's face.

'You don't mean we're going to fly to Sydney in that?' she gasped.

'It's perfectly safe,' he assured her. 'A Cessna is one of the most reliable forms of transport in the outback, and I ought to know since I've travelled thousands of miles in them.'

'But this is too much!' Serena wailed. 'Going to all this expense when it isn't necessary. We aren't that far away from Sydney, surely? I won't have you going to all this extra expense and straining your resources. I don't want to be wrapped in cotton wool. I'm not an invalid. I can travel and lead a perfectly normal life within reason while my back heals.'

She might just as well have talked to the plane, for Bren was urging her forward with strong fingers on her arm. When she hung back he scooped her up and put her in the plane. The interior was cosy, with four passenger seats upholstered in turquoise leather and a space behind for the luggage. With great expertise Bren clicked her seat belt fastened and tucked a rug around her knees. Serena gave a sigh. With Bren one had to say nothing and simply let him take charge.

'Where's the pilot?' she could not resist saying, for he had closed the door and shut them in.

'You're looking at him,' he answered dryly.

'You? You mean this is your plane?'

'That's right.'

'But I thought you were a grazier?'

'I am.'

'Then you aren't poor at all. You must be well off to own your own plane.' For the last few minutes Serena had been opening and closing her mouth in a mixture of surprise, consternation and now what could be called a slight sense of shock. Sadie had hinted that he was well off, but even so, to own his own plane, and for him to tell her that his neighbours were far wealthier than he was——! She had imagined Tamura to be a similiar station to the Cockatoo, which was not so big by Australian standards.

She spoke her thoughts aloud indignantly. 'Why, you double-crossing, arrogant, deceitful Aussie, pretending to be poorer than your neighbours!'

He grinned and prepared to take the controls. 'Steady now,' he murmured lazily. 'Those are strong words to use to your husband.'

'You are not my husband! I suppose you own half the outback too.'

'You'd be surprised,' he said mockingly.

Furious, she retorted. 'Nothing you do would surprise me.'

'I shouldn't be too sure if I were you.'

Serena was steadier now. At least this was movement and she was getting somewhere away from Bren.

She asked, 'Why did you pretend to be poor? You lied to me.'

'I did not,' he contradicted.

She protested. 'You did. You said your neighbours were wealthier than you.'

'That's right.'

Serena glared at him. 'Define wealthier.'

Bren smiled at her from his seat at the controls, and her heart tilted.

'Some would say it's a matter of values defining wealth. For myself, I don't reckon wealth as such in material things. In my opinion a man who has a loving wife and a happy family is the wealthiest man in the universe. My neighbours have loving wives and happy families. I haven't.'

She said more calmly, 'Then why haven't you married?'

'I wanted a wife whom I could love above all other women.'

'But you had to mould her first into your conception of what you wanted her to be?'

'Not exactly. She had to qualify in the first place for the role.'

'You mean vital statistics and all that?' Serena asked, thinking that Sadie qualified in every way.

He laughed. 'Lord no! This isn't exactly the place for such a conversation. I might tell you some day. Maybe we'll both learn something from this mock marriage of ours that will help us when we have the real thing.'

He reached out for the controls and she wanted to shout at him. She wanted to tell him that he was lucky, lucky to come out of the whole affair unscathed while her world would be in ruins. Unbelievable that she should be torn asunder with her love for him and he should be so unaware of it.

Tremulously, she wished that the plane might crash and that they could end their lives together. Indeed, there seemed to be a likelihood of it happening, for the plane, so terribly small and frail, left the ground to waver at a frightening angle before straightening out. Then they were off, and Serena began to enjoy it. The flight to Sydney would not take long and with luck she might even get her old flat back. Katy would be glad to see her.

Not like Bren, who was obviously glad to see her go. He had been quite lighthearted since boarding the plane. But she must not grudge him his happiness. He was a nice man, his sense of values was right, and any wife of his would be gloriously happy. In a way she was sorry he was proving to be so nice, for he was making it harder for her to forget him when the time came. Meanwhile she would enjoy the few blissful hours they would share together before they parted.

The sky was a brilliant blue and she closed her eyes. When she opened them again they were flying over scrub, then a river, a gleam of silver threading its way through leafy glades. To her right presently she saw the tracks leading to a cattle station where paddocks were filled with grazing cattle.

The plane droned on, more scrub, then the river again this time through a densely wooded area. The landscape was now gradually softening into greener pleasant lands and a backbone of low undulating hills. To Serena, who had been expecting to see the approaches to Sydney by now, it was extremely puzzling.

'How much longer?' she asked.

'Not long.'

The landscape became more rural and the hills continued in a low guiding wall. Then came a long stretch of green and the plane began to lose height. They were approaching neat paddocks with the hills and the river never far away. Cattle roamed and buildings appeared at intervals, reminding Serena of the dwellings where the stockmen lived on the Cockatoo station.

She suspected nothing until her eyes picked out the airstrip set in flat green planes of parkland dotted with scrub. Near by were neatly kept sheds and cattle yards. Then a homestead, a gem of a place with a verandah around the ground floor designed in arches of iron filigree delicately wrought. In the centre of the façade two stories of high bay windows jutted out topped by their own slanting roofs over the porched entrance. The second storey of the house had two semi-circular windows jutting out from the verandah around it. These each had a separate roof shaped like tall pointed Welsh hats. Tall chimneys adorned the rest of the deep eaves. Serena was enchanted.

'What a darling house!' she cried. 'Are we stopping here to refuel?'

'Like it?' Bren asked carelessly.

'It's fabulous. Everything is so green and well kept.'

'Glad you like it. Care to look over it?'

He was already sliding out of his seat at the controls and with surprising agility, he was out of the plane and lifting her on to the air-strip.

Serena was glad to move after sitting for so long. She looked about her as they stood for several seconds, noting that they were about five minutes' walk from the house.

'I had no idea we were so far from Sydney,' she prattled on. 'When we went to the hospital for the X-rays I gathered it was on the way there.' Her face was bright, her eyes eager. 'We must be quite near Sydney by now.'

Bren took her arm, said lazily, 'Think you can walk to the house? After being in bed for two days your legs might be shaky.'

'I'm all right. I wasn't ill—just the slight concussion. If it wasn't for my back I would be . . .'

She broke off and he lifted tantalising brows to slant a glance down at her sudden telltale colour.

'Go on,' with a sardonic lift of his mouth. 'Where would you be—or should I say where had you intended to be? You have admitted not intending to go with me to Tamura.'

Serena bit her lip. 'Well, I wouldn't be on my way back to Sydney, would I? I'd probably be away on my travels again. By the way, how far are we from Sydney that you have to come down for refuelling?'

'Who said anything about refuelling?'

He met her look in his usual direct fashion and the expression in his eyes sent her heart beating quickly enough to send little tremors through her. She stood still, noted unconsciously that they were only a short distance from the house, and repressed qualms that all was not right.

'You mean friends of yours live here and we've broken the journey for a break? It's very kind of you, but I would much rather have gone on to Sydney so I can get fixed up with somewhere to stay.'

He spoke after a brief pause with disarming gentleness. 'I've already fixed you up with somewhere to stay. You've just admitted that you like this house, so what's wrong in staying here?'

She stared at him, striving against a strange agitation. In a voice hardly above a whisper, she said. 'This is Tamura, isn't it? I think I knew when I first saw it. It was a beastly thing to do, to deceive me into coming here.'

'I didn't want it this way.' Bren sounded hard now, his voice rasped. 'What else could I do? You didn't want to come. I meant to talk to you about it. I actually saw us having a laugh over coming here. You stand a chance of getting better here much quicker instead of going to Sydney to slog away in an office. It was partly my fault that the accident happened.'

The heat of anger in her voice made it husky. 'You can't explain a doublecross. You've spoiled something rather fine between us. How can I ever trust you after this?'

'Don't be silly. I'm the same man that you trusted when we spent the night in the same room. I've done nothing to make you doubt me in any way. I never said I was taking you to Sydney—you took that for granted. You'll enjoy it here, make new friends and build up many happy memories to take back home with you. Why,' he said whimsically, 'I'd like to bet you won't want to go back when the time comes for you to leave.'

Serena trembled inwardly. Prophetic words that stabbed like knives in her heart. She had lifted her head to gaze at him like a startled fawn. Colour was flooding back into her face and her silky hair blew in feathery strands across her eyes. She brushed them away and tried to speak, but no sound came.

He said, very quietly, 'I'm going to pick you up in my arms and carry you the rest of the way to cross over the threshold. By way of continuing our little farce try to look like the happy bride. I suggest you put your arms around my neck in order to keep your back straight.'

There was something forceful yet unreadable in his expression, and for a moment Serena hesitated. Then with admirable calm she lifted her arms to place them around his neck as he lifted her. Her eyes, however, were trained towards the house and the woman coming out in the bright sunlight to greet them.

Bren was saying rather quickly, 'I've had one of the downstairs rooms turned into a bedroom for you. No sense in risking a jolting to your back by using stairs. Besides, I've stressed the fact of your needing to sleep alone until your back is better. So there'll be no awkward situations to slide out of or awkward questions about our sleeping in separate rooms.'

He stopped short within earshot of the woman smiling at them so warmly.

'Here we are, Binny,' he cried with his charming smile. 'Darling, this is Mrs Binns. Binny, my wife, Serena.'

Conscious of being in Bren's arms, Serena uttered a polite greeting, feeling a kindred spirit as their hands touched. The woman was about ten years or so older than herself, well made and slender. Her eyes were a flecked hazel, her nose slightly retroussé, and her mouth, generous to a degree, turning up humorously at the corners. Her hair was cut short and the sun struck red lights in the brown. She chuckled at Bren.

'So you've brought back a present for Tamura this time, and what a beautiful present, if I may say so. The boys will be tickled pink!'

Serena laughed with a touch of uncertainty. 'What a lovely compliment, Mrs Binns! I never thought I would be referred to as a beautiful present for a homestead, and never one as lovely as Tamura,' she exclaimed with that winning friendliness that few strangers could resist.

'Tamura is beautiful, isn't it?' the other woman said, completely won over by Serena's friendliness. 'I'm sorry you had an accident, Mrs Robart. Bren asked me to prepare a downstairs room for you for the present. The small lounge at the far end of the corridor, I think you said? It has a lovely view of the paddocks and hills. Of course, when you go upstairs the view is really something.'

Bren carried Serena into the house, across the hall and turned to the left along a corridor. A door was open at the far end and he strode in to deposit her gently down on her feet.

'How is your back?' he asked.

'Fine. I told you there's nothing to fuss about. Do you have any newspapers this far out?'

He cocked a brow in surprise, said politely, 'Australian papers, do you mean?'

'That's right.'

He pushed his hands into his pockets and said crisply, 'If you're thinking of looking for a job in Sydney it's off. You never give up, do you?' A pause. 'Still determined to leave?'

She ignored the interrogative note in his voice. 'If you don't interfere, we shall get along fine. What's more, I'm only taking care of the future by seeking a job in the next place I plan to visit later. No harm in that.'

'I agree, only don't make it too obvious, will you, in case Binny or anyone else around thinks it odd that my bride should be already seeking a job.' Bren smiled. 'After all, we're still at the honeymoon stage which we're supposed to take later. There'll be the party too that I promised at the Cockatoo. But first things first. I'll go and fetch your luggage.'

Serena stood there waiting for Bren to return with the air washing over her like a fragrant shower. There was a feeling of being far out of the universe where everything was vast and untouched. She was here at Tamura, Bren's home. Resentment against no one in particular, unless it was Bren, heightened the loneliness. But was not loneliness a healing balm sometimes—a time to reflect on which way our life was leading—a time to sort out the chaff from the wheat? Besides, was not this a more comfortable way to see the country, with good meals and a bath on hand whenever it was wanted?

The room was beautiful and restful, with the bed an added necessity. The ceiling was high for coolness, the windows high and giving a splendid view of the hills. The bed had been placed beneath one of the wall lights, a single divan with a beautiful lace bedspread over apricot silk. A bedside lamp had an apricot shade—touches of femininity presumably new in a delightful room which was obviously a small lounge. Could it have belonged to Bren's mother? There was an exquisite writing desk, a small bookcase containing leather-bound books, several comfortable chairs and a delightful French clock with revolving golden balls on the mantelpiece. It was not hard to imagine his mother using it for a small sitting room where she might have planned surprises in the past for birthdays or anniversaries.

It would probably be Bren's wife's room when he married, she realised faintly, and gave a start as he strode into the room with her case. His dark eyebrows lifted in mock surprise to see her still standing where he had left her.

'Welcome to Tamura,' he said with a pained smile. 'You don't have to ask permission to move around, you know. I hope you'll be very happy here.'

He placed the case on one of the bright thick rugs covering the floor and snicked it open. Then without any preliminaries he scooped out the contents and placed them on the bed.

'Can't have you straining your back by heaving this suitcase around,' he commented practically as he snicked it shut and picked it up as though to carry it away.

'Thank you,' Serena murmured haltingly, and added. 'Where are you taking it?'

'In one of the linen cupboards in the corridor,' he answered. His unwavering glance, his baffling tone put her very much at his mercy. She put her hand nervously to the open neck of her tailored blouse where a pulse was beating chokingly in her throat, and he noted the gesture with narrowed eyes. 'Hell's bells!' he cried explosively. 'Stop looking at me as if I'm your jailor! You're free to come and go whenever you choose, but not back to Sydney. Under-

stand? I won't have you returning home with the idea that
I've ruined your visit here to this country. If there's anything you want you have only to ask. Binny has the softest
heart in the outback and I can assure you that you have
nothing to worry about. Don, her husband and a lifelong
friend, is equally soft.'

Serena drew in her lip. How could she explain to him that
her fear of herself was far greater than her fear of him?
Her treacherous heart leaned towards him each time he
appeared. It was going to be harder and harder to keep up
a cool, careless attitude in his presence. She was ashamed
of her own emotions, ashamed of the fact that she was in-
experienced in life.

No wonder Bren was impatient with her! He was so used
to Australian girls who were quite free of her kind of inhibitions. Even now he was mocking her girlish silence
with those deep penetrating eyes that missed nothing.

She was forced to retaliate, but not unpleasantly. 'Thanks
for everything,' she said in a low voice. 'You must give me
time to adjust. After all, you plonked this on me out of the
blue when I was all ready to land in Sydney and pick up
where I left off. Now that day has been put off, but not for
long, so you can be sure I shall make the most of my short
stay here.'

'Having quite a shake-up, aren't you?' he drawled, strolling to the door with her case. 'First your fall, then this
unexpected hop to Tamura.' He turned to flick a cursory
glance over her slim figure. 'Don't worry, you'll survive.
See you later.'

Serena stood staring for several moments at nothing after
he had gone. Then with a deep sigh she proceeded to put
her clothes away into a wardrobe placed against a wall in
between the two tall windows. The task was done when
Mrs Binns knocked on her door and Serena told her to
come in.

'Everything all right?' Mrs Binns wanted to know cheerfully. 'You know, I'm still wondering how Bren met you.
You're new to this part of the country, aren't you, and

you're definitely English, with that accent.'

Serena regarded her for a moment, rather taken aback. Then she laughed.

'Bren picked me up in the street in Sydney,' she said mischievously.

'He didn't?' Mrs Binns cried in amazement. 'That doesn't sound like Bren, and it doesn't tie up with you either.' Then quickly, 'I'm sorry, I shouldn't have said that. It isn't any of my business, is it? The truth is I'm over the moon because Bren has had the good fortune to meet someone like you. I do hope you won't misconstrue my curiosity and regard it as impertinence. I only hope you won't miss your former life in the U.K. too much.'

Serena laughed again. 'Bren can make life so much fun I'm sure any problem of that kind will never arise. Any girl who marries a man not of her own country should be content to live with him in his.'

She found the truth impossible to resist, partly because this very friendly person would not be easily deceived and partly because it was her love for Bren talking. The latter fact hastened her to add rather quickly,

'Don't betray my confidence to Bren, will you? I should hate to have him think he has me in the hollow of those strong brown hands.'

Mrs Binns looked at her, and a tender look came into her eyes.

'Of course not. You'll want someone to confide in until you make your own circle of friends, and I'd like to think I could be that someone until you do. It was very interesting to hear you could ride.' She looked with appraisal at the smart moleskin jodhpurs Serena was wearing after being taken to the hospital in them. 'You're more than half settled in already. There's a shower across the corridor facing your room—Bren had it installed to save trailing dirt upstairs. Supper will be ready in half an hour. Will that be all right? I suppose you'll want to make some alterations. It's only natural.'

Was there a tinge of regret in the woman's voice? Serena

hastened to reassure her. The last thing she wanted was to disrupt Bren's household when he was going out of his way to help her in return for her helping him. Mrs Binns was probably a first-rate cook, used to catering for the hungry stockmen and for Bren. So she was much too valuable to lose, especially as Sadie did not look the kind who would be happy to slave in the heat over a cooker.

'Oh no, please,' she pleaded. 'There are to be no alterations at all, and they would never affect you, Mrs Binns. You see, I have to take things easy for a while on account of a slight injury to my back. While it's only slight it might take weeks or months.' She laughed again. 'I've never had any back trouble before, so I can't say.'

'You mean you have to take care?' sympathetically.

Serena nodded brightly. 'I can do most things, but nothing rough like riding that could interfere with the healing process. That doesn't mean I'm to be treated like an invalid, though. Bren is apt to treat me in that way, and you mustn't follow suit.'

Mrs Binns said understandingly, 'I can understand Bren being anxious. He wants you to get better. You'll find he's very considerate and he'll take great care of you in every way possible. I always said he would spoil any wife he had by killing her with kindness. I'm glad you aren't the kind to coddle yourself.'

Serena found herself lost in momentary confusion. She had forgotten for a moment that her marriage to Bren was no real union, and Binny was obviously thinking that it was.

'Are you all right, Mrs Robart?'

Serena blinked at the look of concern in the other woman's face and pulled herself together.

'Yes, of course,' she answered brightly. 'Thanks for all your kindness. I'll be ready in half an hour. I'm looking forward to a shower.'

Mrs Binns moved to the door. 'We're lucky to be near the river and there are several springs quite near which help. Sure you can manage?'

Consideration was one of the woman's qualities and Serena was very grateful that her stay would be made more tenable by it. Mindlessly, she told herself that that there was something to be said for knowing the set-up. Anyway, who cared, since it was only a temporary situation? So she smiled politely.

'No cosseting, Mrs Binns. Please,' she said gently.

Half an hour later she was having supper with Bren. Mrs Binns had made it a special occasion by placing a candelabrum in the centre of the table and using the best china, glass and silver. The dishes were placed upon the table and Bren served from them. The food could not have been better prepared and Serena found herself eating with enjoyment while keeping her eyes lowered on her plate most of the time even while he talked.

The light from the candles flickered a bronze mask over his clear-cut features. Mrs Binns had said he was kind, would be too kind to his wife. Yet Serena knew from the expression in his highly intelligent eyes and the set of his well-cut mouth that he would not tolerate a woman holding the reins in his household.

He might have descended from English stock, but the Australian blood was very potent in him, all the same. They moved into the adjoining lounge for coffee. Bren's head was thrown back against his chair, his long legs were thrust out in front of him and his strong lean body was relaxed in the comforting hug of well-sprung upholstery. He gave the impression of not having a single care in the world, and Serena told herself bleakly that she was responsible for his obvious contentment; she had told him that Sadie loved him.

Sick at heart, she looked round the pleasant room. At the far end the dining room was visible through an archway that showed the dining table beneath a tall window looking out over the garden. The decor in there and continuing in the lounge presented a scene of muted colours, soft autumn tints echoed in the cushions, curtains, and upholstery, giving a visual impression of space.

Behind her two comfortable sofas were set at right angles to form the basis of a get-together for any guests who would arrive to talk in a comfortable group. There was also a baby grand piano, shelves of books and the usual modern equipment of record player and tape recorder. Occasional tables were glass-topped and the flower arrangements added a homely touch. To Serena it represented a much lived-in sitting room, thoroughly comfortable and ever-welcoming.

'This is a very comfortable room,' she said. 'Your Mrs Binns is a treasure.'

He smiled wickedly. 'You mean the little woman's touch in a man's world. Australia is a man's world. What's more, our women prefer it that way.'

'Good for them,' she returned tartly. 'But they have little say in the matter, do they, being so isolated?'

'Not so isolated as you imagine. We keep in touch with civilisation and we have a flying doctor service linked with the finest hospitals in the world.'

The tell-tale colour rushed to her face as their eyes met. There was a hint of laughter in his and to hide her confusion she said quickly,

'I'll never understand why you continued to see me in Sydney after picking me up in the street.'

He laughed softly. 'Come now! For a pretty girl you're surprisingly modest. You promised to be a pleasant interlude in a lonely grazier's life. You are now, if you relax and accept it as such.' He frowned and added, 'I can't say I like the way you describe our first meeting. I picked you up from the pavement, but I rather gathered that we were introduced, roughly I admit, by unruly teenagers. So no more talk of pick-ups. Come on, I'll show you around the house.'

Serena's feelings were mixed as she followed him on a tour of the house. Once again he had hinted that she was only there on a visit and she did not care for him continually reminding her of it. As if she was likely to forget!

There were six bedrooms and four bathrooms, with the

main bedroom extended to include a dressing room and a bathroom. The main colour scheme was a soft apricot off-set by gentle shades of green with a pretty Kashmiri rug on the floor. The thought that one day Bren would be sharing the room with his bride made Serena shy away from it quickly. The tour of the house was bitter-sweet, but she did enjoy it and soon became lost in admiration and surprise as some particular object caught her eye.

She walked gracefully with Bren from room to room. The quiet tinkling laugh bubbling in her throat, the dainty expressive gestures of her hands as she hovered above something that particularly enchanted her, rejoiced the eye of the beholder.

Bren moved nonchalantly beside her. His mouth quirked with amusement as he noticed that never at any time did she step beyond the bounds of good manners by becoming too familiar in her reactions. They were standing at the window of one of the bedrooms looking at the view and Bren was watching the frank enchantment of her face when she looked up at him. Their gazes held, clung ... and in turning round too quickly in her utter confusion, Serena struck her ankle against the leg of a chair.

The jarring pain made her feel sick, but she gave no sign of it having hurt her. Unfortunately the injured ankle refused to support her and she grasped the back of the chair to prevent herself from falling.

'What is it?'

Bren was looking down at her in concern and she managed a pained smile. 'It's nothing. My ankle gave way. I'll be fine in a moment.'

'Let me look at it,' he said, and lowered her gently into the chair.

Slowly his fingers explored the slender ankle bones and Serena tried not to wince when he touched the tender spot. His fingers were strong and warm but far too magnetic in their touch. She gritted her teeth as he massaged it slowly, and gradually the pain eased, although she still felt a little sick.

His eyes were upon her now as he continued to massage the fine bones.

'You caught it on the furniture, didn't you?' he said abruptly.

She nodded as he scanned her pale face, and his next words were almost savage.

'Then why in heaven's name didn't you say so, instead of behaving like a martyr?'

Huskily, she said, 'How on earth did I know that the knock would take the use out of my foot?'

He raised a brow, his voice openly mocking. 'Do you mean to say that your mother didn't instruct you in the best art of defence when attacked? Kick anyone in the ankle on that same spot where you knocked yours and they'd be unable to run after you.'

His manner was keen and a trifle teasing, and she relaxed, was able to retort in a similar vein.

'You aren't seeking to put me off continuing on my tour of the country by any chance, are you?'

His eyes narrowed. 'Would it be any use, do you think?'

Serena did not answer. This was dangerous ground on which her feet were slipping. Her gaze lowered to the strong brown fingers on her ankle and it was as if they were holding her heart in a warm tender clasp.

'No answer?' he mocked wickedly. 'Can it be that you're changing your mind about moving on?'

Serena pushed the streaky blonde hair back from damp temples. The moisture there, brought on by a feeling of nausea at striking her ankle, was being replaced by fear—the fear of his magnetism and her overwhelming love for him. A few more intimate situations like this and she would be falling into his arms. It was her own fault. Everything was her fault.

'No,' she said hardily, 'I'm not changing my mind. In the meantime are there any more useful hints you can give me, like massaging the bruised spot to prevent the blood from congealing?'

A dimple appeared in her cheek and his eyes darkened into a gleam.

'Did your mother tell you that?' he asked lazily as his fingers began slowly to caress her ankle.

She nodded. 'Among other things, like not speaking to strange men.'

A moment elapsed before he said, 'Then she wouldn't have approved of you taking anyone who picked you up seriously?'

Serena answered quickly, nervously, 'No, she wouldn't. I'll try to stand now, thanks.'

Bren took his time releasing her foot and lowering it down. Then, straightening up, he gave her no chance to carry out her intention to walk on it.

'Stop being a martyr,' he told her grimly. 'I had intended to carry you downstairs in any case lest you should jolt your back in the descent.'

He was barring her path and giving her no alternative than to give in to him. She braced herself for his arms around her and he scooped her up silently. Serena closed her eyes against his own particular brand of masculine fragrance. It was her heart that spoke.

'What I said just now about not speaking to strange men—I meant nothing against you. I'm very grateful for what you did. As for going downstairs, I shouldn't think it would harm my back. You don't have to feel too responsible for me.'

Bren had dropped lightly down the stairs and she felt hardly any movement as he clasped her firmly. He had carried her to her room and put her down gently on her feet before he answered.

His expression was as remote as snow peaks on hills. 'Maybe I'm being extra careful with you in order to hasten your recovery. The idea of you coming to Tamura was to that end—to put you on your feet as soon as possible. As for being grateful to me, I have reason to be grateful to you anyway. So let's forget it.'

He left her abruptly with a cool goodnight and closed

the door behind him. The hour was not so late, not yet ten
o'clock. Was he going to his office to catch up on some work,
or was he going to telephone Sadie? Nothing wrong in him
doing either, certainly nothing for Serena to be upset
about. He would do just what he wanted to do, and that was
to get her better as soon as possible in order to settle
things between them. He had brought her to Tamura to
keep an eye on her, like someone in a business venture
that just had to come right. Only theirs was a fake marriage
which, ten to one, he was wishing he had never made.

CHAPTER TEN

THE hour was quite early when Serena awoke with the sense of something having awakened her. Her travel clock said five-thirty and the cold air on her face made the bed more tempting in its warmth. But a sense of foreboding was hardly conducive to sleep, so she swung her legs out of bed, and reaching for her wrap on a nearby chair, slipped into it. A dark mauve sky met her gaze as she peered through the window. It was not yet light.

No use asking herself the wisdom of rising so early with nothing to do. Just as silly as asking herself what she was doing here in the first place. But she was, and this was her first morning at Tamura. While Serena Downs would never belong here there was no reason why she should not make the most of every minute of her stay. She had never been one for staying in bed, and if one had a sense of adventure one was never squeamish about rising early in the cold.

She was dressed when Mrs Binns tapped on her door. 'I heard your bath water running, so I assumed you must be up. Would you like a cup of tea?' she said kindly. 'I'm on my way to get breakfast for the boys.'

Serena beamed. 'Better than that, I'll come and help you to make it.' Her spirits rose. With Binny it was easy to talk and behave naturally. 'Bren took me over the house last evening, but he didn't show me the kitchen quarters,' she added chattily.

Mrs Binns said dryly, 'Maybe he aimed on keeping you away from anything that means work. He's anxious for you to get better!'

The kitchen was at the back of the homestead, a high-ceilinged, streamlined affair dominated by a refrigerator with built-in cupboards and all the latest electrical gadgets. None of the fierce heat of the sun nor the dust storms would penetrate this air-conditioned domain. It was a house-wife's dream.

With the expertise of having everything at her fingertips, Binny was busy switching on the kettle and taking milk from the refrigerator.

'You take milk, Mrs Robart?' she asked.

'Yes, please. No sugar.' Serena reached for buttercup yellow cups and saucers from the kitchen dresser and placed them ready. Then pausing with a sense of being a fraud by way of her new title she added, 'Call me Serena, will you, Binny? And I do want to help. What about helping in preparing the breakfast?'

'Who mentioned breakfast?'

The owner of the voice materialised and Serena was hearing Bren's voice raised in anger outside her room at the Cockatoo as he told his jackeroo to beat it back to Tamura. Kerry had not lost any of his swagger, the swagger of a man who knows only too well that he is popular with the opposite sex.

'Good morning, Binny, Mrs Robart,' he said, eyeing Serena with blatant appraisal. 'Nice to see someone around decorating the place. No offence, of course. The boss obviously thinks you're still in bed since he sent me to order you breakfast in bed. No doubt he told you he intended to have breakfast in his office before he sets off on the daily grind?'

Serena smiled as if she knew all about Bren's plans. 'Are you going with him?' she asked politely while Binny made the tea.

'No. I take things over here at Tamura while the boss is away. So anything you want to know, I'm at your service, at all times. Should you need me at any time I'm never far away.'

Binny had prepared a tray, covered it with a cloth and placed it in Kerry's hands.

'Away with you and take Bren his tea before it gets cold,' she told him briskly. 'And not a word, mind, about Mrs Robart being up and in the kitchen.' When he had gone, she added. 'That young man would be more likeable if he worked with his hands half as much as he does with his tongue, not forgetting the eye-play for the women. He's a real one for the girls.' Her smile was bright as she poured out tea. 'Now let's discuss ways and means of keeping you occupied without overdoing it over a cup of the best.'

Those first few days at Tamura began to take a serene leisurely pace with Binny putting her into focus with the routine of Tamura. Binny told Serena that most of the graziers' wives did their own chores, kept open house and made their friends welcome at any time. For the moment there was a limit to what Serena could do. Her work in the kitchen was limited since Binny had to keep to a tight schedule in order to keep everything running like clockwork. So it was decided that Serena could move about as she felt inclined, doing light tasks like arranging flowers in the house or feeding the orphaned lambs and calves.

One of the jobs she enjoyed was dusting the rooms, and especially Bren's office. The comfortable swivel chair of padded leather worn by his presence, the ashtray he used, presented a masculine sanctum the timbre of which set up all kinds of curious vibrations inside her. How she would have loved to work there! But she did not dare ask him if she might, since common sense told her he would hardly welcome temporary help that would be sorely missed when she left Tamura.

Everything in the kitchen seemed to run on push-button efficiency, with sizzling chops, sausages, steaks, fried eggs and fresh bread along with butter, marmalade and steaming cups of tea to begin the day. Tamura produced its own meat, milk and eggs, with some produce from the kitchen garden. Once a week the mail delivery van brought stores and fruit from the city.

That first morning Serena had watched Bren take off in the Cessna. She had watched him hop in, close the door, start the propeller, and heard the engines roar as they flashed. The plane began to move, gunned fast, to taxi along the air-strip and off the ground in a lightning take-off. It lifted, dipped, circled, then levelled off. The next moment it had gone.

Serena had stood transfixed, hands clenched and a prayer in her heart for his safe return. But he did not return that night nor the next. He came through on the bush telegraph and spoke to her in loving terms with the knowledge that they were on a party line. Maybe only Serena in her hyper-sensitive state of being hopelessly in love with him could detect the mocking cynicism of his endearments.

Bren returned in the afternoon of the third day. Two wedding presents had arrived and Binny was about to take the parcels along to his office on his instructions when Serena volunteered to take them. She was looking around at the shelves in his office for a place to put them when the sound of a plane droned on the quiet air. Her heart lurched with the knowledge that Bren had returned and she sank down into a chair as her legs went weak. In a way she wished that he had not come back yet, wished it so much that tears sprang to her eyes like grit. This living as it were in a vacuum, feeling nothing at all while he was away except the ache for his return was goaded by her own indecisions. Fiercely she told herself to keep her emotions in check. Only by being calm could she solve the puzzle of knowing what to do. Not only was she superfluous here, the whole silly idea had been a mistake from the start.

Rising slowly to her feet, Serena looked up again at the shelves, decided on a space above her head and drew a chair forward to stand on in order to reach up. It took some time to make a space wide enough to take both parcels and she was about to get down from the chair when firm footsteps were heard and Bren entered the room.

Poised on the chair, Serena stared at him as though hypnotised, at the thick dark hair recently released from his hat as it lay in damp tendrils on his forehead, at the lean tanned cheeks and those intent dark eyes that made her incapable of independent action or word.

His look was one of utter astonishment and she felt the

anger coming from him in waves. He was in front of her in one stride.

'What the devil do you think you're doing?' he demanded explosively. 'Don't you know you can jar your back by jumping on and off chairs?'

She stiffened at the grip of his hands around her waist as he lifted her down. His hands, warm and disturbing, deliberately retained their hold as he scanned her face. As though against his will his mood changed. His mouth quirked at the corners.

Softly, he said, 'Done any more foolish things while I've been away?'

Serena tried not to tremble in his hold. Was he aware of his every movement being deliberate, like the way his expressive dark eyes between those thick dark lashes fixed themselves intently upon her, and the deep cadence of his voice attacking her heart head-on? Was it possible that he knew his power over women, over her?

'Such as?' she asked.

'Like missing me.'

Serena deliberately hardened her expression. 'Now that would be foolish, wouldn't it? I guess I've missed you about as much as you've missed me. Incidentally, I suppose Binny told you about the wedding presents that came today from friends of yours? I've just put them up on the shelf.'

His hands dropped from her waist. He did not look up at the shelf.

'They'll be taken care of.' His voice was noncommittal and her prickles rose.

'Aren't you worried about them?' she cried, and to her dismay tears sprang unbidden to her eyes. She lowered her lids to hide them and steadied her voice. 'I feel awful about them. It's—it's—all so pointless!'

'I wouldn't agree. Nothing that achieves its object can be termed as pointless. It's common knowledge that, as my wife, you are temporarily indisposed, making it essential for us to put off any celebrations for the time being. There's nothing to be upset about.'

Serena clenched her hands. He did not care. It was all a huge joke to him. Well, she would play it that way too.

She said, 'What about my helping out in this office? I would feel happier if I earned my keep while I was here.' Her smile was bright and efficient. 'I can do accounts, filing, document records, etc.' Her pause was rent with the desire to shake him. 'I can even print cards. For instance, cards for returning the wedding presents when the time comes.'

He smiled faintly, giving nothing of his thoughts away. 'You came here to rest. Binny tells me you've been helping to feed the orphaned lambs and calves. And there's your photography. What's wrong with filling in your time that way?'

'It isn't enough for me to do. If I'd continued with my plans of touring the country I would have taken the occasional office job with some grazier to help my finances along. I can still do the other jobs I'm doing now. I like being independent.'

Bren's jaw tightened and the icy look he flicked over her gave the sensation of a bad east wind.

'You mean you don't want to be beholden to me?' he said quietly.

Her colour rose and washed through her cheeks. 'I mean nothing of the kind, and I wish you'd stop treating me like an invalid!'

He raised a brow. 'But I don't have to object if you treat me as an employer, do I? I was thinking of us both seeing this place from the same angle, discovering things leisurely. We have a small kind of country club I aim to take you to, introduce you around. That's what you want, isn't it, to explore and meet people?'

His voice was soft, dangerously so. But his eyes were wary as if he was weighing every word before he used it. If he was playing a game then it was one she could not work out.

She nodded. 'Yes, but I refuse to take everything and give nothing in return.'

He grinned disarmingly. 'Careful now! Those are dangerous words to a mere male.' His eyes held hers—the arch enchanter. 'Maybe you'll be safer locked in my office for a couple of hours a day in case your feelings get the better of you.'

'A couple of hours?' she gasped indignantly.

Bren nodded. 'That's what I said. A couple of hours each morning, no more. I'll show you the ropes after supper, and don't push your luck. By the way, I've brought you a present back. I threw it on to your bed on the way here to the office.'

'A bribe?' she said as he reached the door.

He turned. His mouth was a little tight, and he eyed her intently.

'I don't have to bribe you, honey,' he drawled. 'You've been scared of me from the day we met.'

How right he was, Serena thought. She said feverishly, 'You must be joking. Since when have I been afraid of you or any man? Why, I can walk out right now if I want to.' She drew some steadying breaths, and with laughter of a sort, added, 'I might find you detestable at times, but that isn't being afraid of you.'

He surveyed her with such cool disbelief that she became a little unnerved. 'What you need,' he said, 'is a good meal to bolster your morale, and as I have the healthy male's natural need for a meal at mealtimes, I suggest we meet in the dining room in about ten minutes.'

In her room Serena found his present on the bed, a stetson hat like the one she had worn of Sadie's. She felt like crying. Instead she picked the hat up and flung it across the room, then dashed the tears angrily from her eyes.

Bren was there in the dining room to greet her, suave, well groomed and very attractive with his white smile and mocking eyes appraising her slenderness in a cream jersey dress of simple cut. All at once her heart began to beat a little faster and she accepted the aperitif he gave her hoping it would steady her.

'Did the hat fit?' he asked.

For a moment Serena was taken aback. She had not tried it on, having left it on the floor where she had flung it.

'As a matter of fact,' she answered, 'I didn't try it.'

He said wryly, 'You didn't throw it out of the window, did you?'

'No. I threw it across the room.'

'Wishing, no doubt, that it could have been me?'

It was the kind of situation which called for laughter between them, but she was still smarting about his insinuations that she was afraid of him. Also she was alert to tricks. To her consternation her eyes were damp.

'Thank you,' she managed at last. 'It was very kind and thoughtful of you to buy me the hat.'

Bren rose to his feet to break the tête-à-tête as Binny came bustling in with the meal.

'Come on,' he said, leading Serena purposefully to the table. 'I hope you're as hungry as I am.'

During the meal he was at his most charming, bridging unobtrusively the gap between them. He could be irresistible when he chose, and when he did his dynamism was lethal. When he took her along to his office later to show her what he wanted her to do Serena even suffered him bending over her as she typed out a letter for him at his dictation which he wanted to be ready for the post the following day.

It was much later when he suggested a short stroll before bed. He waited while Serena fetched a wrap from her room and they walked outside to the smart white picket fences of the paddocks, crossing a lawn as soft as a carpet underneath. In the gloaming the landscape changed to softer country backed by the low undulating hills. The night was immense, the air knife-sharp, and the sunset lingered as though reluctant to leave.

Tremulously, it seemed to Serena strolling beside him that moments passed on dancing feet. They were alone, withdrawn from the noisy world on a pinnacle of ecstasy and joy. As far as the eye could see the vast ceiling of pearly sky was slowly changing to a mysterious grey blue. Soon it would be dark. Serena wanted so much to stop the passage of time—to make the precious moments go on for ever.

Surely it was worth while waiting one's life for this eternity of time with the beloved?

Drinking in the sweet cold air she felt that this was the true Australia, the land of the pioneer, with Bren as the typical Aussie from the outback, very tall, good-looking, moving with that lazy, easy nonchalance that belied the strong character underneath. Droughts, dust storms, fires, and floods, such men took them in their stride, accepting them as part of the daily round.

To their right the slopes rose gently from the paddocks into a steep hill dotted by gum trees and rocks. The climb was well worth it to see the panoramic view from the top.

'You can take pictures up here for your album,' Bren drawled as they reached the summit to gaze out on to the darkening scene. 'Tamura isn't big compared with some of the other stations around, a mere fifteen thousand acres compared with all of half a million of others around. But it's rich in crop produce and is good grazing ground. When I was a kid gentlemen graziers reared sheep and drank whisky. Growing crops was left to small farmers. Now times are changing. We now combine what's best for meeting the demands of today's markets.'

Serena stared at his proud dark profile, his lean hardness, with the sensation of being caught in a sweeping torrent that without wish or volition of her own carried her swiftly along. There was neither the will nor the wish to resist his deep musical voice. She was carried along on her own wishful thinking that they were not worlds apart and only partners on paper.

'Am I boring you?' he asked quietly as he noticed her long silence, her gift for listening.

'Goodness, no, I've enjoyed every word. I'm even beginning to be glad I came here because I'm learning so much about the country.' The pale shimmer of her face flowed up to him. Her eyes, a deep violet blue in the twilight, shone with enthusiasm. Her soft pink mouth parted to show small even teeth like pearls. She looked young, alive and untouched.

'Ah yes, we mustn't forget the reason you came to this country. I don't suppose you've found it enthralling enough to make you want to stay?'

Something unmasked, hard and compelling in his voice hurt. If he was beginning to worry that she would not set him free when the time came, he need not. Tears tore at her throat. But she only said gently and steadily,

'How can I answer that when I love people and places so much? How can one possibly settle in all the places one learns to love?'

His eyes smiled wryly down on the blur of her face. 'For one who has the frailty of a flower, life flows strongly in you, little one. May all the places you visit be pleasant ones.'

Serena did not answer him. Emotion, born of a rather unusual propinquity, writhed inside her. She wanted to say that anywhere he was would be the only place she wanted to be. But it was no use—he belonged to Sadie, had done all along. They strolled down the hill again and he left her to go to his office after wishing her a quiet goodnight.

She was awakened the next morning by a tap on her door, and Bren came in with a tray.

'Cup of tea and a request,' he said, placing the tray across her knees and sitting down on the bed.

Serena had pushed herself up hurriedly into a sitting position on being awakened out of a deep sleep. She looked tousled and defenceless, with the appealing charm of being embarrassed at his nearness. The line of his jaw went taut.

He said equably, 'The time is only just after five, but I'm taking Binny to Sydney right away. Her husband has taken a turn for the worse in hospital, and I wondered if you'd mind giving Kerry a hand in the kitchen with the boys' breakfasts?'

Quickly, because he was watching her, Serena poured out the tea from the small pot.

'Binny's husband?' she said unsteadily. 'Has he been in an accident?'

'No. He had an operation for appendicitis weeks ago, but they kept him in hospital because of some kind of adhesions. Binny didn't tell you?'

She shook her head. 'I'm so sorry.'

'So am I. He was my right-hand man. I hired Kerry in his place because he hadn't been feeling well for the past year or so. He was doing light work when he was taken ill and rushed to hospital for an operation.'

'Poor Binny!' Serena sipped the hot tea. 'I'll only be too glad to help.'

He nodded. 'Binny has written down the morning's chores, which include the breakfast. I don't know if you can cook or bake, but Kerry will give you a hand. He knows most of it, and mind—no lifting or any heavy work. He'll do all that.'

'I can manage. I have a good idea what Binny does. You don't have to worry about me.'

He said indifferently, 'I'm not. It's Kerry I'm worried about. He's a ladies' man and you're just the kind he goes for. Only with Kerry every girl is fair game. He's not the marrying kind, at least not up to now.' He gave her a swift keen look. 'He might go hook, line, and sinker for you because you didn't swoon at his feet the way girls usually do. So take it easy, will you?'

Serena gave him a startled glance. 'Why should I if you think I can win him over as a prospective husband? For all you know I might have set my cap at him already. I'll admit he isn't a wealthy grazier, but he has the looks that a girl needs to give romance to a possible friendship. You might even be able to name him as co-respondent when we part.'

It was Bren's turn to look startled. 'Hey now, no need to go that far! And no hanky-panky under my roof—understand? You're still Mrs Bren Robart and don't forget it. And don't forget—look after your back.'

'I'll do that. And don't talk as if you own me. I'll cope.'

He gave a slow smile at the indignation in her voice. 'Don't you like to be taken care of?'

'Not for the reason you're doing it, because you want my back to get better quickly.'

'Don't you want your back to get better quickly?'

Serena lowered her eyes from his intent gaze. 'Of course

I do. I can't wait until I'm well enough to continue on my travels.' She smiled. 'Sometimes I feel it's not to be, that I'll never set out doing what I came for.'

Bren said thoughtfully, 'Maybe that's how your friend Dee feels at the moment. Heard from her yet?'

She shook her head. 'Not since I came here. I left word with Katy's mother in Sydney to pass on any mail for me to any address I might give. I haven't given this one to Dee.'

He raised a brow. 'Why ever not?'

'Because I don't plan to stay here long anyway. When my back is pronounced fit you won't see me for dust.'

She felt his hand touch hers lightly on the bedcover, heard him drawl indifferently, 'Well, that's straight enough anyway. Glad you can cope with the present situation.' He rose slowly to his feet and looked down on her speculatively. 'I've discovered through life that fate has quite a sense of humour, so one is better equipped to deal with her many surprises by keeping a sense of humour oneself. So long now. Go easy on the boys—the next few weeks are going to be very busy ones for them.'

CHAPTER ELEVEN

SERENA was an instant success with the stockmen at Tamura. Following Binny's written instructions to the letter, she managed to keep things much as they were beneath her capable hands, and everything went smoothly. She enjoyed her tasks immensely, delighting in the easy friendliness of the men, and revelled in being able to produce perfectly cooked food. She forgot her shyness, and her face was flushed and animated as they paid her compliments on her cooking. And they all pronounced her to be 'a beaut' when they filed out again to work.

As for Kerry, he was a real help, but she did nothing to encourage him. That he was openly amused at her indifference to his charms did not escape her, but he kept his place knowing that he would have Bren to deal with if he did not. Serena thought of the girl named Rose in Sydney who had been so upset because she could not find him and wondered what kind of a game he was playing with her. A closer inspection of his features revealed a rather loose mouth, and an effeminate jawline which betrayed a weakness in his character the rest of his good-looking face belied.

No, Serena decided, Kerry was the last man she would want for a husband. But then she had been spoiled by Bren, or rather Bren had spoiled her for any other man. From now on she would find herself comparing other men who might interest her with his fine qualities and good looks and find them sadly wanting.

No other man would ever make her spine tingle, her pulses race and her senses reel as Bren did. Her life stretched ahead of her, not widening into a heavenly existence with the man she loved but narrowing, dwindling, and shrinking

towards the final acceptance of compromise with someone else.

The evening meal for the boys had been dealt with and
cleared away. Serena prepared the evening meal for Bren,
Binny and herself should they return, then went to have a
bath and change. Around seven o'clock she heard the
Cessna approaching and she went to the door of the homestead to greet them. The plane taxied to a standstill and
feeling curiously shy she awaited Bren's arrival with bated
breath.

But that breath died in her throat and her heart lurched
when he strode forward, not with Binny but with a far more
glamorous figure by his side—Sadie. Some of the light went
out of Serena's eyes as she waited to greet them. Sadie had
her arm tucked into Bren's as he carried her case and she
was talking to him animatedly.

Bren's greeting was skilfully brief. He left Sadie eventually to leap the verandah steps as though carried forward
on a rush of clear mountain air. His very brief embrace was
enchanting, his face cool from the evening breeze, his mouth
cool and fresh on her cheek. Had Serena known that he was
bringing Sadie she would have found something flippant
to say, something appropriate for the occasion. As it was
she was stunned into silence.

She heard herself saying disjointedly, 'What happened?
Binney's husband isn't worse, is he?'

Bren sobered. The brilliant smile he had put on for
Sadie's benefit faded. 'No change,' he answered his voice
noncommittal. 'Binny is staying at the hospital with him for
the present. Sadie is here to help you cope.'

Sadie came forward looking glamorous in a cape and hood
of Scotch plaid. Her eyes sparkled with challenge.

'Hello, Serena,' she cooed, giving her a butterfly kiss on
her cheek exactly on the spot where Bren's had rested
earlier. Serena wondered if it was given in an attempt to
wipe out that first kiss. 'I thought I'd come to help out.
Bren can take my case to the room I usually have when I'm
staying here.'

For the first time Serena noticed the case Bren carried, and she looked up to meet his eyes.

He said, 'We'd like a meal after we've freshened up. Anything will do and we'll have it in the kitchen. No doubt you're worn out with the day's chores, darling.'

She tried not to wince at an endearment which was only a figure of speech. But her smile was bright.

'Oh, but I'm not worn out, and everything is laid ready in the dining room just as Binny does it. Only don't be too long getting changed, will you? I don't want the meal to spoil.'

He looked down at her then, noting the pretty dress in midnight blue which intensified the violet of her eyes, the aura of light around the bright hair and the softness of her lips that gallantly kept up a steady smile. He seemed about to say something, then the moment passed as he went swiftly indoors followed by Sadie.

Serena gave them twenty minutes, then took the meal to the dining room. She had lighted the candles on the beautifully laid out table with a flower arrangement in the centre which she had placed there to set off the silver and glass. On her second journey from the kitchen with the heated containers Bren met her to take it from her.

A bit roughly, he said, 'You don't have to do this. I'll fetch whatever you want from the kitchen.'

Lightly she retorted, 'You don't have to, this is the last, and there's plenty since I provided for Binny as well.'

He inhaled the aroma coming from the tray with the satisfaction of a man with a healthy appetite. 'Smells good,' he commented.

The meal was everything Serena had worked so hard for, the steaks, medium rare, as Bren liked them, the fish pie had pastry light as thistledown, the bread, freshly baked, was golden brown and crusty, the chocolate soufflé was light as air.

Bren sat back in his chair replete with what he said was one of the most delightful meals he had enjoyed for a long time. In the glow of the candlelight he loomed tall, wide-shouldered, and carved in bronze as he rose to his feet to volunteer to make the coffee.

Grinning whitely, he said, 'I must congratulate Kerry on his cookery.'

'Poor Serena! You would have been lost without him, no doubt,' Sadie said as she leaned across the table for Bren to bend and give a light to her cigarette. 'It must have been quite comforting, Bren, to know that you could leave the station in his hands.' Sitting back in her chair, she blew out a line of smoke, insolently it seemed to Serena, who sat quite unruffled at the conversation. 'My dear Serena,' Sadie continued through the smoke haze, 'I bet you never imagined how hard-working a grazier's wife is expected to be. But I suppose you'll learn.'

Bren filled the tray with used dishes and made off for the kitchen without a word, while Serena rose to her feet in the role of the perfect hostess and suggested they moved into the lounge to more comfortable chairs in which to enjoy their coffee.

'My dear Sadie,' Serena interposed as they sat down, 'the average English girl doesn't have to learn to work hard—it comes naturally since boys are usually spoiled from the cradle up.'

Sadie shook her head. 'Even so I doubt if you have the makings of a grazier's wife. You see, Bren can't do without me. He never will. Why else do you think he called at the Cockatoo to ask me to come back with him to help out?'

Serena smiled. 'He could have been concerned for me. He doesn't like the idea of me doing too much until my back is better.'

Sadie's eyes narrowed as she blew out more cigarette smoke into the air. 'I suppose your back is really fractured?'

'Oh yes, no doubt about that. Mind you, it's only a hairline thing. The surgeon said it could heal up very quickly or it might take a long time.' Serena went on smiling. 'I just have to wait.'

Sadie gave the impression of mulling this over, then she said,

'Why not ask Bren to take you for another X-ray at the hospital? You never know, your back might have healed.'

Serena said amiably, 'A good idea, providing Bren will agree to take me so soon.'

'Take you where?' Bren was back with the coffee tray and Kerry in tow.

Serena gave him a disarming smile as he placed the tray on a small low table near to her chair.

'It isn't anything important,' she said as he passed her a cup of coffee.

Kerry greeted Sadie and sat beside her on the spacious sofa while Bren, having served the coffee, took his cup and stood idly against the mantelpiece to look down on them.

Kerry said, 'Sorry to butt in on your first night back, Bren, but I thought you'd want to hear what's gone on during the day.'

Bren drank part of his coffee and said lazily, 'We can talk later, Kerry, when the girls have gone to bed.'

'But not yet, surely?' cried Sadie with a coy look at Bren and then Kerry seated beside her. 'I think a vote of thanks is called for to Kerry for the splendid meal he's prepared this evening. He's going to make some lucky girl a good husband one day.'

Kerry gave a somewhat sheepish laugh. 'Say, what is this? Me domesticated? You must be joking! Love 'em and leave 'em, that's my motto. Of course there's always the chance I might fall in love some day. Stranger things have happened.'

Sadie sipped her coffee, then made an impatient gesture with her cigarette.

'You don't mean to tell me you're going to deny some girl the benefit of all that talent you have,' she retorted. 'You've been hiding your light under a bushel, as the saying goes.'

Kerry looked dazed. 'Let's get this straight,' he began. 'I've no idea what you're talking about. I had nothing to do with the meal you had this evening. In fact, I've done nothing all day except act as a general dogsbody to Mrs

Robart.' He grinned at Bren. 'Your wife cooked your meal and also the meals for the boys. Let me congratulate you on a real beaut of a wife. The girl is wonderful! All that vitality and energy and managing to look glamorous with it as well. The boys are wild about her. You'll have to keep her on a leash from now on, and I speak for myself too.'

In the silence that followed Sadie's hand holding her cigarette trembled so much that she dropped ash on to the carpet, while Bren drank his coffee, looking lean and dark-eyed. Not by the smallest twitch of a muscle did he show how he took this information from Kerry.

As for Serena, she was content to let them think that Kerry had prepared the food. What did it matter anyway? This time next year Serena Downs would be forgotten at Tamura and Sadie would be installed there as Bren's wife.

Suddenly the food and the coffee were tending to send her to sleep. It had been a long day and she was now feeling the strain of it, unaccustomed as she was to a hectic day that had begun at five-thirty that morning. Her eyelids weighed a ton and they insisted upon closing.

'What you need, Mrs Robart, is your bed,' Bren said crisply when she had failed to hear what he had been saying.

'Perhaps you're right.' She smiled up at him as he relieved her of her empty coffee cup. 'See you in the morning.'

It was eight o'clock when she woke the following morning as Bren entered her room with her breakfast on a tray. Guiltily she pushed herself up in bed, flushed with sleep and decidedly tousled.

'Goodness, why didn't someone wake me?' she exclaimed, pushing back the heavy streaky hair from scarlet cheeks. 'I'm awfully sorry.'

Bren strode to the bed to place the tray in front of her. 'Don't upset yourself. You aren't doing any chores in the kitchen today or any other day. Sadie will cope.' He lowered his long length down on to the bed near the foot and looked at her with a narrowed gaze. 'Why didn't you say last evening that you'd cooked the meal instead of letting us think that it was Kerry?'

'It isn't important, is it?' she answered coolly. Tremulously it occurred to her how wonderful it would have been
if Bren had really been her husband and that he had brought
her breakfast after awakening her with a kiss. But he was
not and he had not. But the thought was balm to her sore
heart and consequently her expression was very sweet as
she sipped her fruit juice.

'You made a hit with the boys.' There was a glint in his
eyes. 'They want to know if you have any sisters. Where did
you learn to cook like that anyway?'

She looked down into her glass. 'You can't have a super
cook like Dee for a friend without some of her wizardry
rubbing off on you. We always took turns with the chores
when we went away into the country to train for our pro-
posed trip here.'

Slowly he said with open malice, 'You two really had
something going for you, hadn't you, easy on the eye and
on the stomach too. The poor Aussies didn't stand a chance.'

Serena did not know quite how to take this, but she spoke
with a miraculous calm, and honesty.

'We wanted our tour to be a success and it wouldn't have
been fair to offer services that weren't up to standard as we
worked our way around the country. We never expected it to
be easy, but it was sensible to come prepared.'

Suddenly he was leaning forward as the last of her fruit
drink slid down the smooth column of her throat. 'Tell me,'
he demanded urgently, 'would you be terribly disappointed
if you didn't make it around the country after all?'

Serena put down the empty glass, feeling the immense
weight of his almost threatening sexuality. Her nerves began
to sag. She looked into eyes that seemed to cut into hers.

'Naturally I would. I've looked forward to it for so long,
saved, sacrificed little things, and even given up my job.'

'And you still want to go back home afterwards?'

'Of course.' Serena stared down at the tray, wishing he
would go. It would never do for him to see how his nearness upset her or that her hands were trembling. She de-

cided on attack, and added, 'I can't see why I'm not to help Sadie in the kitchen.'

He said lazily, 'Two women never hit it off in the kitchen!'

Serena dimpled. Her eyes sparkled and her small laugh was like the tinkling of water coming from a spring. Her nervousness was forgotten despite the dangerous glint in his eyes.

'What's the joke?' he demanded.

'Oh, Bren,' she exclaimed, 'you're so delicious saying a thing like that! What do you, a bachelor, know about women?'

'Plenty,' he growled. 'And don't go looking at me like that. I won't have it.'

'Like what?'

'Never mind.' He rose abruptly to his feet. 'You'd better eat your breakfast, and if you want to make yourself useful you can do two hours in my office before lunch. No more.' Although he had spoken roughly something vulnerable in his face caught at her heart. The next moment it was gone as he added on a parting shot, 'And behave yourself too!'

Now what did he mean by that? she thought, picking up a crisp brown roll. Poor Bren, he was evidently finding Sadie's presence frustrating and was wishing their positions could be reversed. Well, the sooner they changed places the better. It could not come too soon. Serena just wondered how much longer she could endure living under the same roof as Bren in the present circumstances. She spent the morning in his office bringing his correspondence up to date. He had listed his instructions, so she followed them, then set about tidying up the room. The wedding presents seemed to mock her from their place on the shelf, and she tried to ignore them. At her request Kerry brought her a glass of milk and a sandwich at lunch time. From him she learned that Bren was out for the day and would be back at supper time.

After lunch, with her swimsuit beneath a comfortable

shirt and denims and her camera slung over her shoulder,
Serena set off for a stroll to the creek. She left the homestead with a sense of relief; only her love for Bren had
magnified her visit to Tamura into melodrama. Meanwhile
there was an enchanting afternoon ahead to fall back and
do the things she had come to do in this wonderful country.

Sadie ran after her as she left the homestead, eyeing the
new hat on Serena's head that Bren had bought her.

With a hint of malice, she drawled, 'New hat? Going for
a stroll?' She wore jodhpurs and was evidently going riding.
Her smile was condescending. 'Sensible girl! You know,
Serena, for all your prowess in the kitchen, not to mention
Bren's office, you aren't the stuff that Aussies' wives are
made of. I expect Bren hardly understood until you actually
came.'

Serena gave her a very straight look. 'As I'm not married
to you I fail to see that it's any of your business. Furthermore, if you're going to take that attitude then the sooner
you leave Tamura the better. I'm sure Bren wouldn't like
you speaking to me like that.'

Sadie coloured guiltily. She gave a short laugh. 'I was only
teasing, you silly. See you later.'

Serena continued on her way determined not to let the
incident spoil her day. In a way she felt sorry for Sadie,
since she knew herself from bitter experience what it was
like to love Bren and not have him. The air was hot but
not humid as she gazed across the paddocks to where the
woods stood out against the hills like dark green silent
islands. The grass was still with little birds swooping over-
head, and willy wagtails hopped on the fences as she passed,
looking hopefully with their bright little eyes for possible
titbits.

In the creek the water rushed from underground springs
and the pool was fresh and inviting. The trees around it
were rather like tamarisks. Some had shiny narrow leaves
that reminded Serena of those of the oleander. Slipping
off her jeans and shirt, she left them with her camera and
swam in the deliciously blue water, floating most of the

time in order not to jolt her back. Later she took pictures of the creek and, after a small chase, a kangaroo.

Then she lay down with a delicious drowsiness in the shade of the trees. How she would hate leaving Tamura. Useless to assure herself that the cities and coasts were more delightful; Tamura and the outback had captured her heart. The shuddering of a horse's coat awakened her. Bren was looking down at her from his horse. Bemused by sleep, Serena scrambled to her feet and shaded her eyes with an arm to gaze up at him. The sweetness of his sudden appearance brought a breathless hush when only the heavy beating of her heart seemed to pierce the stillness.

His mouth lifted at the corners and that irresistibly charming smile creased his tanned features showing startling white teeth against the brown.

'Hello,' she said since he made no effort to break the silence, then coloured as she realised that she was in her swimsuit.

'Enjoying yourself,' he said, dropping down from the horse to tower above her. Then he nodded at her camera on the ground by her clothes. 'Like me to take a picture of you to put in your album along with the others?' He bent down to scoop up the camera at the ready.

'In—in my swimsuit?' she stammered.

'Why not? You go in and out at the right places—deliciously so. I suggest you move back a little and lean against that tree growing from the side of the creek there. That's just right. Hold it!'

He clicked the camera, then frowned down as he wound the film. 'Seems to be the last one.'

Serena made no answer. She slipped on her jeans and shirt hastily before that keen gaze slid lazily over her again. There had been nothing offensive in his look. It had been almost impersonal. He gave her the camera and she said impulsively,

'Have you heard how Binny's husband is?'

'No change,' he replied. 'I'm going over tomorrow to the hospital to see him.'

'Can I go with you to have my back examined? It would be a good idea to see how it's faring. Don't you agree?'

Evidently he did not, for he frowned. 'Too soon,' he said laconically. 'Take it easy, partner. You're doing fine.'

Serena bit her lip in exasperation. 'I'm not your partner, except in crime!'

She had to laugh then at the startled expression on his face. But he was not amused.

'Where's the crime come in? You're getting all het up. You could enjoy this if you'd let yourself.' He eyed her intently, noting her flushed face and harassed air. Then he bent down to scoop up her hat before she could do so. 'How's the hat?' He placed it on her head. 'Not bad, but you still don't look Australian.'

'Why should I? I'm English. Nothing will ever change that.'

She lifted her chin defiantly and he made a playful feint beneath it with a bunched fist.

'I shouldn't be too sure of that if I were you. Like a lift back?'

'No, thanks, I prefer to walk.'

'Suit yourself.' He swung up on his horse and looked down at her soberly. 'I couldn't very well take you with me tomorrow and leave Sadie alone with Kerry.'

With that parting shot he wheeled the horse around and rode off.

That evening Kerry waited on the table. Later he went to Bren's office with him to discuss the following day's schedule. Serena followed them and went into the kitchen to wash the dishes; she thought it was the least she could do after Sadie had done the chores all day. From there she went to bed leaving Sadie and Bren together.

Bren left at five the following morning. The sound of the plane leaving awoke Serena. She was dozing off again when Kerry tapped on her door to say that Sadie had a bad head so could she come to the kitchen to prepare the breakfast.

She was glad of the activity and took a tray along to

Sadie's room when the boys had gone. Sadie greeted her rather sullenly, said she would stay in bed until lunchtime by which time her headache would be gone. But Sadie did not get up until Serena was preparing the evening meal after the boys had had theirs in the kitchen.

She certainly looked better for her stay in bed and had obviously spent hours on getting herself dressed for the evening. With her dark hair piled up on top of her head, she wore a figure-hugging silk jersey dress in a pastel shade of lilac. Her necklace and bracelet were in chunky silver with matching mobile ear-rings.

Serena thought if she had dressed up to impress Bren the time had not been wasted. In fact she began to wonder if the headache had been genuine after all. And she had timed it nicely to fit in with the business of preparing the supper. Everything had been done, even to laying the table, when she glided into the kitchen.

Serena was still dressing when Bren arrived and Sadie greeted him at the door. To her surprise Binny had come with him. Her husband was out of danger and was responding to treatment. Tears came in Binny's eyes as she told Serena about it after calling to see her in her room on the way to her own. But soon she was smiling now that he was out of danger.

She said brightly, 'I'll be right down to get the supper when I've changed. We have two guests, two boys on their way home on holiday from university. Bren gave them a lift. He takes them on home in the morning. Their parents manage a station of Bren's up north.'

When Serena went downstairs to supper the two guests were already in the dining room with Bren and Sadie. They were about twenty years old, both blond, both tall and lanky. They greeted Serena shyly and were intrigued to discover that she was English. Soon they were calling her Serena, and she was calling them Derek and Paul. For most of the evening she answered their eager questions about London. They had been six when they had emigrated to Australia with their parents, and had been promised a trip back home, as they called it, when they finished their studies.

When they retired to the lounge for coffee the two boys had somehow managed to seat Serena between them on one of the sofas set at right angles to each other for comfortable get-togethers, leaving Bren and Sadie to sit on the other. It was not long, however, before they were all talking to each other and around ten o'clock Bren suggested they all have a short stroll before it grew too dark. Again the boys commandeered Serena. Apparently they knew Tamura well, having stayed there often during school holidays when they were young, so it was not surprising that they should become separated from Bren and Sadie.

They strolled to the creek and Serena learned from them that the trees she had found intriguing were athel and Cook trees, the latter growing poisonous seed pods. But the moment was fraught with too many agonies for Serena to take it all in. Somewhere in the gathering dusk nearby Bren was strolling with Sadie—a Sadie who was dressed to kill. Useless to tell herself that her pining for him was hopeless. Tonight Bren had looked more attractive than ever. He had set himself out to put the two boys instantly at their ease, had encouraged them to satisfy their enormous appetites and to behave as if they were indeed at home.

They knew Sadie well and her chic appearance made little or no impression upon them. It was Serena in whom they were interested, and they were thrilled to know that Bren, their idol, had married one of their kind. It was late when they went to bed, Serena only going to her room after offering Binny help in settling the two boys into guest rooms. But Binny had everything under control in her capable hands and Serena went to bed with the feeling that she did not belong, never would.

She was struggling with a reluctant zip on her dress when the peremptory tap came on her door and Bren entered.

'Having trouble?' he asked, taking in the situation at a glance. Soon he was behind her and she could feel his cool fingers against her skin below her bra as he attempted to get the thing going. At last he did it, sliding it down easily to the base.

'Want me to turn my back while you put on a wrap?' he asked politely.

He did so and she slipped into a housecoat after grabbing it from a chair.

Bren's voice was cool and amused as he moved across the room to lean back against the dressing table to face her.

'Don't look so embarrassed, little one,' he drawled. 'I'm not an ogre who eats little girls up late at night. I dropped in to tell you that I've had a word with the surgeon at the hospital about your back and he suggests that you come along with me the next time I go to the hopital. I'm afraid I shan't be going again for about a month since Binny's husband is now responding to treatment. When I do go it will be to bring him home.'

Serena swallowed hard on her disappointment. She said, 'Thanks for asking the surgeon to take a look at me. Perhaps when I do go my back will be better. After all, they weren't too sure about the fracture. The line was very faint on the X-ray.'

'True,' he said carelessly. 'What do you think of the Brown brothers?' he added. 'You'd like their parents. I suppose they told you they were Londoners. They're the kind of immigrant this country wants, not afraid of work.'

'I liked them very much.' She tightened the cord of her housecoat nervously around her trim waist. Bren's long cool look of appraisal had a touch of cynicism about it which she did not care for. 'I'm glad some of the English meet with your approval.'

He said lazily, 'I wasn't aware I'd said they didn't.'

'You never miss an opportunity of letting me know that I don't fit in,' she retorted.

There was a wicked gleam in his eye. 'You should worry, since you're only aiming to stay long enough to see the country before hitting the trail back home.' His eyes narrowed on her flushed face. 'What did you mean when, during a conversation with Sadie the other evening, you said something about me being willing to take you somewhere?'

'It was nothing important.'

'But I might want to take you,' he insisted.

She raised her eyes and looked directly at him. 'You are taking me in a month's time.'

He raised dark brows. 'The hospital?' His grin was white. 'She evidently wants to be rid of you.'

'Yes, she does, doesn't she? That's as good a nightcap as any you've had since you decided to teach her a lesson. Now I'll say goodnight.'

He straightened indolently. 'Thanks, partner,' he drawled lazily. 'I wish your nightcap was as comforting. Sleep well.' He strolled to the door, then turned for a last word. 'By the way, I'm off early in the morning to take Derek and Paul home. Wouldn't like to come with me, I suppose?'

'You mean you can't very well ask Sadie unless I come along too?'

'It's an idea, although it wasn't the general idea. What do you say?'

Serena smiled. 'I'll come on one condition—that you don't overdo the loving husband bit. I won't have you putting Sadie through the hoop while I'm present. I have a thing about hurting people even though they might deserve it.'

CHAPTER TWELVE

SERENA had never known a month to go so quickly. The future stretched out before her like an impending doom. Bren had played his part in taking her about and showing her the country, but it had not made things much better. She enjoyed the trip to Lyndhurst station that the Browns managed for Bren, and spent a pleasant day with them. Mike and Angela Brown had made as much fuss of her as their sons Derek and Paul had done, and they were only a few of Bren's friends who welcomed her wholeheartedly into their midst.

One day Bren had taken her and Sadie to the Country Club, a short car journey from Tamura. It was fairly compact, with a bar, a games room, a dance room, and tennis courts. Serena had made friends easily with the locals, being avidly interested in all they did. She even took photographs during the journey, much to Sadie's amusement.

Sadie's presence at Tamura had been a strain in more ways than one. Not only had Serena to be careful about making the girl suspicious about her relationship with Bren, she also had to endure seeing her with Bren. Although Bren behaved normally with his lost love there were times when he went for short strolls with her in the evening before bed when Serena had made some excuse and gone to her room. After all, it was what Bren wanted that counted, and he wanted Sadie, she had thought. The week before they were to go to the hopsital, Bren sent Kerry off on a new job to a friend of his with a station in Darwin. Since it was as good a post as the one at Tamura, Kerry was quite happy to go. He left on the mail truck which was to set him down at the nearest railway station, and they all saw him off. Bren, wide-shouldered in bush shirt, moleskins, and big hat

pushed at the back of his thick black hair, shook his hand,
thanked him for his services and wished him well. Binny
pushed a large lunch box under his arm and he kissed her
cheek. His parting with Sadie had been flippant and cool,
but he had stood for several seconds looking at Serena as
she offered her hand. Then with a pained smile he had
shaken his head.

'I'll never understand why guys want to emigrate from the
U.K. when they leave dolls like you behind,' he said. Then
he bent to kiss her hand.

'That was nice,' Binny remarked as they all went back
indoors. 'You obviously bring out the best in Kerry, Serena.'

Sadie was saying something quite different to Bren. 'Now
confess, Bren, that you sent Kerry away because you were
just the tiniest bit jealous of him having an affair with me?'

Bren had grinned down at her with his eyes twinkling
wickedly on the backs of Binny and Serena as they followed
them indoors.

'Does the thought make you happy?' he asked in deep
penetrating tones.

Sadie thrust her arm through his. 'Perhaps just a teeny
bit sad as well. Thinking on what might have been.'

'You never know your luck,' was his instant reply, and
Serena, walking within earshot, felt any slender hopes she
had nursed of meaning anything to Bren disappearing as
if they had never been.

Binny's husband continued to make good progress and he
was now well enough to talk to them through the bush
telegraph. Binny was over the moon as the day drew near
when he was to come home to Tamura. Sadie was travelling
back with them to the Cockatoo; Bren was to make a slight
detour and drop her off on the way to the hospital.

The previous night Serena had gone to her room soon
after supper to pack her bag, leaving Bren and Sadie to take
a last walk before going to bed. In her room she pictured
them together with their arms around each other talking
about the future when they would be free to marry. Serena

had no doubt that having kept Sadie under his roof for a month, Bren was sure to tell her the whole story behind his marriage.

Snapping her case open, Serena began to place her things in it, stony-faced. Well, at least Bren would be happy with the woman he wanted, for there was no doubt that Sadie would have him like a shot. She recognised his tap on her door and swung round as he entered. Immediately he saw the case his mood changed. He had walked in with tousled hair as if he had been running his fingers through the thick mane. His eyes had looked strangely dark. Now they glittered oddly, and his mouth set.

'And what are you supposed to be doing?' he asked, closing the door and leaning back against it with folded arms.

'What do you think? You come barging in here as if you have the right to open the door without a by your leave, then demand to know what I'm doing. I would say it's perfectly obvious.'

She smoothed out the folds of an evening dress with fingers that shook despite her calm exterior, and suddenly Bren was there, taking the things out of the case and putting them back on to the bed.

'You're not leaving tomorrow. You're only going to the hospital for a check up, after which you'll come back with Binny's husband until you know the results of your examination.'

He clicked the case shut and swung it to his side by the handle.

'But you can't forbid me to go just like that,' she croaked. 'If my back is better there's no reason why I shouldn't continue with my plans and do what I set out to do.'

'You won't know whether your back is better or not until the results come through.'

'I can wait,' she insisted.

'You will come back with me. You can look after Binny's husband during the flight.'

'But he won't need looking after. He's been walking about

the hospital grounds for some time—he told Binny so on the telephone.'

Bren strode to the door with the case. The face he turned to her was grimly set.

'We had a pact, remember? Right? I aim to break it amicably and in the right way. We'll discuss it after we have the results of your X-ray. Goodnight.'

When he had gone Serena sank down on the bed and closed her eyes. He could only be planning to send her off like Kerry with a cheque for her services and maybe put her on the train for her next destination. And there was nothing she could do about it, short of leaving him after the X-ray, and she couldn't do that and leave him to take Binny's husband back alone.

After all, the man might be more sick than he would have them believe, and Binny could have come with Bren herself to collect him had someone stayed behind to look after the boys. She was resigned to it the following day when they left Tamura in the Cessna. Sadie said little during the journey and it was a great relief when they dropped her off at the Cockatoo. Julia was there to wave them off again and they were soon at the hospital.

The X-ray went off all right and she was introduced to Dan Binns. He was a man nearing forty, pleasant-faced, broad of shoulder, but he had obviously lost weight. His rugged face was lined too much for a man of his age. But his smile was content enough and he was able to walk to the plane unaided. Bren looked pleased enough to sing at the top of his voice when at last he took off on the homeward journey. He tucked the rug about Dan's knees as carefully as he tucked the one around Serena's.

In fact the atmosphere in the plane seemed to Serena to be one of blissful happiness because three people were returning home when there were really only two. Five minutes with Dan Binns and she felt as if she had known him all her life. As he confessed how the grumbling appendix had dogged him painfully for twelve months until the happy release via an operation, Serena likened the pain to her own love for Bren. Would there be a feeling of release for her after they had parted for ever? If only it could be so! But there was no cure for love unrequited, not the kind of love she felt for Bren. It came but once in a lifetime.

Dan was all in when they arrived at Tamura. Concerned, Serena suggested he used her room to lie down for a while to save him going upstairs. Binny and Bren supported him between them to the room on the ground floor and Serena, fetching her housecoat, went to use one of the bathrooms upstairs. It was only when she had wallowed for ages in the luxurious scented bath in one of the guest rooms that she remembered she had brought no dress upstairs with her to change into. There was nothing for it but to go down to her room and get a dress from the wardrobe.

Hoping not to disturb Dan, who would probably be sleeping off the effects of the journey by now, she went carefully downstairs in her silk wrap. As she reached the hall Bren came striding across to her from the direction of his office. He had changed into a dinner jacket in honour of Dan's return and looked very tall as he moved with a wide-shouldered grace towards her. As he saw the silk wrap his well-defined mouth lifted slightly at the corners.

'Serena?' He paused as he spoke her name and lifted a dark tantalising brow. 'Tut, tut! Don't tell me you aren't ready and the supper all waiting?'

She pushed back the blonde streaky hair from a suddenly flushed face with a small pale hand. How she hated him taking her unawares! He seemed to take advantage of it as he looked her over with searching grey eyes.

With as much dignity as she could muster facing him as it were undressed and without make-up, she said, 'I forgot to take my dress with me to the bathroom upstairs. I hope I shan't disturb Dan when I go in to fetch it.'

He said coolly, 'I wouldn't if I were you. Binny has taken their supper in. Later they're going upstairs to their room. You're all right in your wrap. Besides, supper is waiting for us and I'm going to do the honours for a special occasion.'

'A special occasion?' she echoed, looking up at him.

But his fingers were on her arm, walking her forward to the lounge where the fire was burning brightly to combat the cool evening air.

'I must say this is very odd,' she protested. 'You in evening dress and me in a housecoat. I feel terrible!'

'You don't look terrible. In fact I rather like your tousled look. I have some news for you. News has just come through that your X-ray is clear—the hairline fracture is no more,' he drawled lazily.

For long moments Serena just stared at him trying to take it in. Then she suddenly cupped her cheeks in her hands. 'Oh, goodness! You mean I'm all right now and I can go on with my plans for seeing the country?'

'Yes and no,' he said.

She dropped her hands from her face and stared at him. 'What do you mean? Yes and no?'

'Yes, you are now fit. No, you aren't going away.'

'Not going? I'll show you if I'm not going!' Her voice trembled despite her anger. There was something in his voice which frightened her. 'You just can't go back on your word. You can't!'

He placed his hands on her shaking shoulders and said quietly,

'Why are you so afraid of me, Serena?'

She pushed his arms away to turn on him fiercely. 'I'm not afraid of you!'

'Then why are you trembling? And why did you push me away?' He stepped back and gestured to the sofa. 'Sit down. You'll have to be very convincing if you want me to believe you don't want to stay.'

But Serena stood where she was, shaking her head and biting hard on her lip to stop the tears that persisted behind her eyes. When she did not speak Bren bent his head towards her and murmured, 'I still think you ought to sit down.'

But she only shook her head harder. 'It's very nice of you, Bren,' she said in a small voice as two tears dropped down her cheeks. 'But you don't have to do anything more for me.

I know my being well means a lot to you in the circumstances.'

'Of course it does. It means we can now turn our mock marriage into the real thing.'

He gave her his handkerchief and she dabbed her eyes. 'I don't think that's very funny,' she said as she wiped her nose.

'It wasn't meant to be. You must know how I feel about you.'

Wide-eyed, Serena stared at him, then gave him the handkerchief back without being aware of doing so. 'You —you mean you love me?' she breathed, still refusing to believe her ears.

'You never guessed? Not even when I kept asking you if you'd like to stay in Australia?'

She shook her head dumbly as he drew her close.

'Then I shall have to convince you, my darling Serena. I'm afraid it's going to be convincing, because I've waited far too long to claim my rights as a husband.'

And it was. The kiss was that of a famished man who needed the sweetness of her lips to sustain him, and Serena clung, giving herself in return.

'Phew!' Bren sighed at last when they both came up for air. 'Who said the English were a cold race?'

She burrowed her face in his neck. 'I wish you'd told me how you felt about me when we married.'

'How could I? You wouldn't have believed me. I tried not to believe it myself at first. I met you when I was at a loose end in town, and I told myself that the electric attraction between us was because you were different from the girls around, with your English accent, your wild rose complexion, your girlish good manners, your evocative quiet laugh and your natural sweetness. I'll never forget how I felt that day I called at your apartment just as you were leaving, and knowing that I might never see you again. I knew then that you were the only one for me. No one could ever take your place in my heart.'

She kissed his neck. 'Not even Sadie? You're not going to

tell me you wouldn't have married her in the end.'

'I'm not saying I wouldn't, although I had plenty of opportunity to do so long before I met you. However, marrying Sadie would have been just another wedding of the kind the man made when he chose the girl who could lift a bag of mealies.'

She lifted her head. 'I haven't forgotten how you taunted me about not being the kind to be a grazier's wife. You said I didn't even look Australian. And you always acted with perfect decorum, always the gentleman. In fact I never thought I attracted you at all sexually.'

He kissed her lips, then moved his mouth to her neck. 'That's where you're wrong,' he murmured. 'Do you recall that morning I came into your room to bring you early morning tea and I asked you not to look at me like you did? You were lucky I went out when I did. I almost jumped into bed with you.'

'Why didn't you?' she whispered against his lips.

Ardent moments passed, then he said, 'Is that an invitation?'

'I don't think you need inviting,' she breathed.

'You mean right now? Without any supper?'

Serena trembled deliciously as his hands slid down her body to lift her in his arms. Her hands slid around his neck.

The vestige of a smile passed over his face as she said, 'What do you think?'

Then he bore her away.

It was much later when Serena snuggled up beside him in his bed.

'Darling,' she said, 'I hope you don't think there were ulterior motives behind my offering Dan my room and forgetting to take a dress with me to the bathroom?'

Bren turned from lying on his back beside her to take her in his arms and covered her face with slow kisses.

'You should worry,' he murmured contentedly. 'Everything I've done since meeting you has had an ulterior motive behind it, like getting your name on a marriage certificate and bringing Sadie to Tamura to make you jealous. Not to mention,' a throaty chuckle, 'getting rid of Kerry double quick when I saw how he ogled you.'

'Really?' Serena laughed softly in delighted surprise. 'I can see I shall have to watch you carefully in the future!'

'For the rest of our lives,' he said as his mouth wandered to the corner of her lips.

'Thanks for warning me,' she said on a bubble of pure joyous bliss. 'I only hope that any ulterior motives you have in the future will be to my advantage as well.'

'You bet they will, since we're in this marriage business for keeps,' he assured her.

'Are we?' Serena teased. 'Doesn't it bother you that I might not be able to lift that bag of mealies?'

His answer was to silence her by a long kiss. Eventually he said,

'Mealies or no mealies, you're mine for keeps.'

Tears brimmed in her eyes. 'Oh, Bren, I do love you! I love Australia as well, but I love you most of all.'

With all her love for him shining in her eyes Serena lifted her arms around his neck and as their lips met she blessed the fates that had brought her to Australia—and Bren.

In 1976 we introduced the first 100 Harlequin Collections—a selection of titles chosen from our best sellers of the past 20 years. This series, a trip down memory lane, proved how great romantic fiction can be timeless and appealing from generation to generation. The theme of love and romance is eternal, and, when placed in the hands of talented, creative, authors whose true gift lies in their ability to write from the heart, the stories reach a special level of brilliance that the passage of time cannot dim. Like a treasured heirloom, an antique of superb craftsmanship, a beautiful gift from someone loved—these stories too, have a special significance that transcends the ordinary. **$1.25 each novel**

Here are your 1978
Harlequin Collection Editions...

Original Harlequin Romance numbers in brackets

ORDER FORM
Harlequin Reader Service

In U.S.A.
MPO Box 707
Niagara Falls, N.Y. 14302

In Canada
649 Ontario St.,
Stratford, Ontario, N5A 6W2

Please send me the following Harlequin Collection novels. I am enclosing my check or money order for $1.25 for each novel ordered, plus 25¢ to cover postage and handling.

☐ 102	☐ 115	☐ 128	☐ 140
☐ 103	☐ 116	☐ 129	☐ 141
☐ 104	☐ 117	☐ 130	☐ 142
☐ 105	☐ 118	☐ 131	☐ 143
☐ 106	☐ 119	☐ 132	☐ 144
☐ 107	☐ 120	☐ 133	☐ 145
☐ 108	☐ 121	☐ 134	☐ 146
☐ 109	☐ 122	☐ 135	☐ 147
☐ 110	☐ 123	☐ 136	☐ 148
☐ 111	☐ 124	☐ 137	☐ 149
☐ 112	☐ 125	☐ 138	☐ 150
☐ 113	☐ 126	☐ 139	☐ 151
☐ 114	☐ 127		

Number of novels checked @
$1.25 each = $ _____
N.Y. and N.J. residents add
appropriate sales tax $ _____

Postage and handling $ ____.25

TOTAL $ _____

NAME _____
                    (Please Print)
ADDRESS _____
CITY _____
STATE/PROV. _____
ZIP/POSTAL CODE _____

AB ROM 2238

Offer expires June 30, 1979

And there's still *more* love in

Harlequin Presents...